The Last Ghost Dancer

The *Last Ghost Dancer*

TONY BENDER

Thomas Dunne Books/St. Martin's Press  New York

This is a work of fiction. All of the characters, organizations, and events portrayed in this novel are either products of the author's imagination or are used fictitiously.

THOMAS DUNNE BOOKS.

An imprint of St. Martin's Press.

THE LAST GHOST DANCER. Copyright © 2010 by Tony Bender. All rights reserved. Printed in the United States of America. For information, address St. Martin's Press, 175 Fifth Avenue, New York, N.Y. 10010.

www.stmartins.com

Library of Congress Cataloging-in-Publication Data

Bender, Tony, 1958–
    The last ghost dancer / Tony Bender. — 1st ed.
        p. cm.
    ISBN 978-0-312-59230-1 (alk. paper)
    1. Spiritual biography—Fiction.   I. Title.
    PS3602.E465L37 2010
    813'.6—dc22

                                    2009047578

First Edition: July 2010

10 9 8 7 6 5 4 3 2 1

For: Gare Bare, Katie, Al Cat, Woof Dog,
Whitey, Witte, Jaye Bird, Mary, Rietta, and Hawkeye

I wonder now if we had never seen a sunset, if an artist's hand rendered it in oils for us in our caves of ignorance, would we believe such a thing could exist? Or would we dismiss it like Plato's Atlantis, like the canals on Mars?

—*Bones*

ACKNOWLEDGMENTS

This story could not be told without those who believed in it and in me. First and foremost, thanks to my wife, Julie, for her unwavering faith in me, and to my children, Dylan and India, for their love and inspiration. I am grateful to my agent, Connie West, who believed in this book from the beginning. Likewise, I am thankful for the encouragement I received from my friend Joseph Marshall III, a Lakota author and scholar, who authenticated the voice of Joe Big Cloud in this book. Finally, thanks to my editors, John Schoenfelder and Karyn Marcus, at Thomas Dunne/St. Martin's Press for their patience, and especially to Thomas Dunne himself for making all this happen.

PREFACE

There is a place in southwestern North Dakota called Pale Butte. You won't find it on a map and only a few people know about it. Let me explain. My good friend Harriet Howe named the butte after reading my manuscript for this book. And if you knew Harriet Howe, you would know that is about as official as it gets. She pointed it out to some of her high school science students during a field trip one day.

The town in this book, Pale Butte, was originally a nod to White Butte, the highest spot in North Dakota, 3,506 feet above sea level. It's curious that the name of that mountain helped inspire a book while the book itself inspired the naming of a mountain. We have come full circle. But even before Pale Butte became a real place, it was alive in my mind like nothing I have written before or since. It consumed me. I dreamed about it. Indeed, a dream I had when I was living in Jamestown, North Dakota, in 1983 is part of the story.

I dreamed of the apocalypse, which is not necessarily the end of the world. It is a Greek word meaning *lifting of the veil* and Greek shorthand for apokalupsis eschaton or *revelation at the end of the age*. It was a dream so powerful it stayed with me. I saw a place in that dream that I had never seen before in a remote area in the Rocky Mountains.

Fate, destiny, and my 1983 Mustang brought me to Denver and the Rocky Mountains for the first time not long after that. Sometime in 1984 when I was driving deep in the mountains I came upon the very place I had dreamed about.

If I had ever doubted that dreams could be tangible things, this experience erased such doubts forever. It was as if the corner of a veil had been lifted, granting me a glimpse of another place and another time.

From the time I was a child, I felt the presence of those some might call angels or guides. In the dream, I recognized my most constant guide, a tall Indian. It was the first time I had seen him, but I had always felt his presence and felt protected.

I am not the first to have such an apocalyptic revelation. There are all sorts of predictions and myths from culture to culture, from the Maya to the Hopi to Nostradamus to Edgar Cayce to Ruth Montgomery. A recent vision from a Sioux holy man that was shared with me was as unsettling as my dream. The atmosphere seems to be crackling with energy and the news that things are going to change in a big way, and, I believe, in the end, for the better.

Many of these predictions conflict with regard to severity and timing, but I wonder if that isn't because we have the capacity to steer things with prayer and positive thinking. I have always believed that thoughts are things with an energy all their own.

You may have had visions and premonitions of your own. If so, here is proof that you are not crazy, or at least that you're not alone.

Originally, this book was envisioned to be a coming-of-age saga drawn deeply from my own life experiences. I grew up in a small town of about four hundred, very much like the Pale Butte in this book. I have said many times that I had a Tom Sawyer existence, and that remains the best description of those years. It seems to me that small towns produce big characters.

However, the characters in this book belong to Pale Butte alone. Now and again they may echo the best qualities of those I have held in my heart or wispy reflections of incidents and events from long ago, but that is all they are—echoes and reflections.

As a matter of geography, the Pale Butte in this book is located in western South Dakota, just along the North Dakota–South Dakota border. In the Dakotas, anything that lies west of the Missouri River is considered "west river." Almost immediately after you cross the river to the west, the landscape changes, becoming more arid and monochromatic, more rugged, with pronounced buttes. It is where the West begins and still endures.

This book, an old man's recollection told from the future, speaks to friendship and the enduring quality of love.

It is a testament to loyalty and sacrifice and miracles and hope. These things are as necessary as the food we eat and the air we breathe.

The story itself was a revelation. It came to me from beyond this place. Each morning at five I would sit at the keyboard with a hot cup of coffee and eventually electricity would begin to vibrate within me, which is the sign that those wiser than I are speaking. I accept the fact that I am an imperfect receiver. You should, too.

Beyond that, I cannot define this story. Nor should I. I just know it was important to tell it. During the time I was writing, the signs and omens were so thick, nothing surprised me. They served as a constant reminder to keep going.

You would do well to watch for the signs as you read. If you are observant, you will see them. You may think them coincidences or anomalies in the beginning, but after a string of them, you will recognize them for what they are. A message from beyond and a reminder that what we see is only a fraction of what there is.

All paths lead to God.
Of course, some have more detours than others!

—*Joe Big Cloud*

The *Last Ghost Dancer*

PROLOGUE

There was a pulse, a groove, a palpable crackle in the atmosphere that summer.

Perhaps it was a peculiar alignment of the planets or sunspots or fate or some sort of cosmic collision of souls. The sun exploded off the pale velvet green of the buttes west of town in a way it hasn't since. The colors were more vivid, the dank smells wafting off the river more pungent.

I don't think it is some trick of memory. I've learned since to better recognize the energies that tug and push us this way and that, and I've learned to not fight it but to trust in it. But back then, I had not seen enough seasons and did not recognize the ebbs and flows, the invisible tides, external and internal, that lift us up or swallow us. Back then, it was just a gnawing feeling somewhere in the back of my brain that I knew something—*something important*—but could not remember exactly what it was. I feel that way quite often these days, but mostly it is just the toll of the decades and not a hidden prophecy or divine insight that has me scratching my head in bewilderment as I try to peer past the shroud that is my consciousness into the subconscious where clarity, ever elusive, resides.

It's like driving at night. You can only see so far ahead, and on cloudy nights when the moon glow is hidden, you just see the yellow lines clipping past and new ones looming. You trust there will always be new lines and more road ahead, but you can't really be sure. Whitetails grazing blacktop can send you into a panicked swerve. There might be a car stalled in your lane right around the curve. Spring flooding might have washed out the road completely.

When you're younger—I don't know if it's faith or ignorance—you drive like hell into that invisible future and God, you feel strong.

In my early years, I had not walked enough trails or experienced enough ugly surprises on the blacktop at night to understand. It was dumb animal instinct that had me on edge with anticipation that summer. It was not the wisdom that comes with scars and scabs and bumps and bruises and worse.

But something was in the air. I could feel it.

It was as if God poured four hundred of us into that small west river town the way I used to shoot all five balls into the pinball machine when I got bored, just to watch them bounce around like crazy. Bells would ring, the bumpers would clatter, and the numbers whirled trying to keep up while I flipped spastically to keep all the balls away from the drain.

It caused some consternation in the Mecca Bar some mornings when the regulars would be there at 10 A.M. with a tap beer in a Hamm's glass and a throbbing temple from the night before. I'd get looks, and sometimes Grumpy Mindeman would groan, hold his head, and wait for the misery to stop. It usually didn't take long. It was suicide pinball. But once in a while, gravity suspended, things would bounce just right, and you could keep the cacophony going full roar. That's how I picture it. Like God was flipping all of us around, bouncing us off each other, just to see what happened.

LUCKY MAN

Woof leaned over his shot, scoping it in as if the cue had a sight, when I walked into the Mecca Bar that Saturday morning. It had rained the night before, and puddles steamed in humidity rare for this western South Dakota climate.

Summer rains offered a reprieve from the business of cutting hay until early afternoon, so the lobbies of the grain elevator and the Farmers Union gas station filled with farmers and ranchers eager to take a break, and the bar and the café did brisk business.

Butch hovered to the left beside the foosball table, staring at Woof's predicament, leaning on his stick, slowly chalking the tip. Sprinkles of blue chalk fell to the green-and-white checkerboard floor.

I glanced at Bob, who was leaning over the cooler to watch, his elbows resting on the scarred mahogany bar. Bob raised an eyebrow. Playing pool with Butch was a risky endeavor—especially if you won. He wouldn't just kick your ass then and there, but he'd seethe and eventually he'd find an excuse—usually after about fifteen beers—and then you were a dead man.

And Woof was just the type of guy who could really wear on you. He had this confidence, this way of looking at you, and you just knew he was always a step or two ahead of you. And Lord, if you messed with him, he would make you miserable. In a lot of ways, it was worse with him than it would have been with Butch. With Butch, you knew what was coming. You were going to get your ass handed to you and that was that.

With Woof Schwartz, the worst thing was the waiting. He would plan. He would set you up, and then the punishment would be worse than your actual crime against him. Psychological torture is what it was.

But at the moment, it didn't look good for Woof. He had five balls to go, and Butch had just one, perched six inches from the side pocket. One miss and it was over, and Woof wasn't the kind of player who could typically run the table. He played an exasperating brand of pool. It was hard to tell if he was playing defense or if he was just inept. Inept and lucky. He'd slide the cue ball into an impossible position, and he'd frustrate the fastballers, the guys like Butch who could shoot the lights out—the guys who loved to slam the ball into the pocket like they were punching you in the ribs.

All the while guys were wishing they had studied trigonometry, so they could figure the angle on a four-cushion bank shot, Woof would slide his balls closer to the pocket, waiting, looking like he didn't have a clue or a chance. It was irritating.

Even I could give him a pretty fair run. But get Woof in there with some shark, and he'd rise to the occasion. The next thing you know, they'd played five games, and Woof had won three, each win looking like some sort of New Testament miracle. He was always the underdog against guys like Butch. But he won more than any underdog I ever saw. I never did figure out if he had an angel on his shoulder or if he was just better than he let on. I never knew for sure. I still don't.

After two more exchanges, Butch was still trying to get a clean shot at the 13, which had been bumped to the far end of the table, almost against the rail. The cue ball was resting against the back rail, and the problem with a shot like that is you can't get any English on the cue ball and if you just blast away, bad things can happen.

Of course, that's what Butch did. Goaded into blasting away out of frustration—he pounded it, and he made the shot—one heck of a shot. But on the rebound, the cue ball headed toward that 8 and clipped it, sending it rolling toward the corner pocket. It crawled. Crept. Moseyed. And there was a chance it wouldn't fall in and cost Butch the game.

You could have smoked a cigarette waiting for that ball to get there. When it did, it seemed to pause at the edge of the pocket as if to contemplate its options. Then it tumbled in, clicking softly as it nestled in with the other balls.

Now, if you were watching for the first time, you might figure Woof got lucky and maybe that was the key. He was lucky. But it sure happened a lot—especially when there was money on the line.

Butch stared his thousand-yard stare and fished in the front pocket of his pearl-buttoned cowboy shirt and pulled out a ten with a hand the size of an Easter ham. He was beginning to realize he'd been hustled. Woof tried to look humble as he crumpled the bill into his jeans pocket, but he winked at me as we headed toward the door. We both heard the angry *thwack* of a cue slamming topside against the rail behind us.

Woof sighed, and I think he knew he had a problem brewing. He was a sturdy guy but not big, and if it was going to come down to an ass-kicking contest with Butch, well, we both knew how that would turn out.

"You know, Woof, most folks when they commit suicide, they use a pistol or a rope," I said. "But I have to admit, overdosing on pissed-off cowboy is original."

"Aww, the bigger they are . . ."

"The deader you are."

Thwack! The cue hit the table again just as we hit the door. This time I thought I saw Woof flinch. He sighed, shrugged at me, and pushed open the door.

It was like stepping from a cave to the surface of the sun. But I was eager to create as much distance from Butch as possible. My carelessness almost ended my life, and that would have ended this story right here. Or at least there would be someone else doing the telling, and they probably would get about half of it wrong.

Woof grabbed me by the scruff of the neck and pulled me back just as Ella Peterson screamed by in her powder blue '67 Corvette. She dang near ran over my toes.

Ella, who was pushing ninety—years and miles per hour—was so old and bent over, she could barely see over the dash, so she just peeked through the steering wheel as she terrorized the town. I looked at Woof and he looked at me, the way you do out here when you've had a close call.

"You have aspirations of being a hood ornament or what?" he asked.

"Well, I won't get hurt nearly as bad as you will if you mess around with Butch. Or have you forgotten what he did to that steer last Fourth of July?"

"Oh, this is the part where you tell me about how Butch bulldogged a steer to death in the rodeo?"

"Hey, it happened. Five hundred pounds of hamburger in the dust."

"Aww, it was a hundred and five that day. Stupid cow probably died of heatstroke."

"I'm telling you, he snapped the animal's neck."

"Sure. And he shot a man in Reno just to watch him die."

It was then I noticed Spook watching us the way a cat eyes a mouse before pouncing. I don't know who gave him the name, but it fit. He seemed to be more specter than flesh and blood. There was always a sense of menace around him.

At burials he watched from the shadows of trees. It was creepy.

"I thought they were going to put him away for good this time." I said.

"The witness recanted."

"He always seems to pick the forgetful ones."

"They get real forgetful once Spook's old man has a talk with them."

"I guess all that skin under her fingernails didn't mean a thing," I said.

"As it turns out, Spook was rescuing the Douglas girl from the real culprit," Woof said. "She was hysterical. That's why she scratched him. It was all just one big misunderstanding. Just like the misunderstanding with Ginger Leesburg way back when. The word is old man Douglas got a pile of money to forget the whole thing. That's why they left town. To start over."

When I looked again, Spook had disappeared.

"You know . . . sometimes I wish . . . I wish that day . . . it was me that got to him first," I said.

Woof looked into the distance. "I think about it, too. If Tiny hadn't been there, I wonder if I could have finished it."

"You would have been doing us all a favor."

We were a block removed from the Mecca Bar when I suddenly realized my opportunity. "So can I have that twenty you owe me?"

"Got ten."

Now, I didn't exactly soar to the top of algebra class,

but I had this problem pretty well worked out. "You just won ten from Butch, right?"

"Uhh, huh."

"So that means you should have had ten to bet."

"Should have. Can't dispute that."

He smiled, handed me the ten bucks, and turned his pockets inside out. Gray lint and a wrinkled Juicy Fruit wrapper rolled out.

"Geez, you could have lost you know," I said.

He seemed to sincerely consider the concept, outrageous as it was. "I dunno, maybe me and Butch could have worked out a payment plan."

By then we were in front of the drugstore. "I could use a milk shake," he said. "Pool sharkin' is a thirsty business. C'mon, I'll flip you for it."

"Nah, havin' lunch with my folks in fifteen minutes," I said.

"C'mon."

"Hell, you're broke, anyway."

"I'll owe you."

It was heads and he won. Naturally.

EDSELS DON'T FLY

The salty-sweet smell of ham tickled my nostrils as I stepped into the screened porch and from there through the front door. My father was poring over a crossword puzzle. The morning's elevator grain dust was already thick on the shoulders of his gray work shirt. He held a pen in his right hand and a cigarette in his left, as he waited for lunch. Oblivious to me and immersed in the vowels and consonants, he didn't look up. Playfully, I clipped him on the shoulder with my fist, knocking a precariously long ash right into his coffee.

"Got dammit!" he growled, dropping the pen and producing a formidable fist.

"You wanna go a few rounds?" I taunted, surprising myself with a passable Ali shuffle. "I *am* the greatest!" I bragged, shadowboxing, now fully possessed by the spirit of the Louisville Lip. "Float like a butterfly, sting like a bee!"

"Olivia, bring me the flyswatter!" Dad ordered, with a Sonny Liston scowl. "Got a bug problem in here!" Mom materialized with a platter of ham in one hand, a bowl of boiled potatoes in the crook of her arm, and the swatter in the other hand. I retreated to the other end of the table when Dad snatched the swatter and began to wave it menacingly.

"I am *sooo* pretty!"

"Come here so I can whack you one."

"You will take a dive in five and it's no jive! I'll make it three if you mess with me! I'll take you down in one just for fun!"

"Champ, tell your brother it's time to eat," Mom said, feigning exasperation at the impending brawl. I shadowboxed all the way to the back porch. It was a damn fine retreat and entirely sensible. My father had forearms as thick as railroad ties.

I found Coop stroking Charlie Brown's ears. Charlie gave me a feeble wag of his stub tail, but he did not raise his head from Coop's lap.

"Hey, bud. Time for chow."

"I want to stay with Charlie."

"He'll be fine. I think he looks better today."

"Really?"

"Sure. Hey, slugger, here's the plan. . . ."

He followed me out, grinning. When he got to the dining room, he began to point at Dad. "It'll be a thriller when I get the goriller in Maniller!"

Mom sighed, Dad grinned, Coop prayed, and I passed the ham.

My father was a stern, no-nonsense kind of guy, but

he would soften when Coop was in the room. Though he was a year and a half older I always felt like his big brother. He'd had a pretty tough go of it. He was born oxygen-deprived. A blue baby. Later they discovered heart problems and a long string of other ailments. In the beginning we were not sure if he would survive. It was hard.

My parents spent long hours in hospital waiting rooms in the early years. There were nights they lay awake, listening for his next breath, waiting for a morning that seemed impossible, waiting for the light as if sunshine could stall death.

I remember praying for the next rattle from his pneumonic lungs while a Dakota blizzard filled the street with chest-high drifts, marooning us forty-seven miles and a lifetime away from the hospital in Boonesville. I heard the concerned murmur of my parents' voices. Softly, softly they spoke, heads bowed in silent prayer.

There were heart surgeries. A patch to correct a lazy eye. Casts to remold clubfeet. A hernia. And other broken parts I have forgotten. The eventual diagnosis was Williams Syndrome. It's a rare genetic disorder. But when Coop was born, doctors didn't even have a name for it. They just called him slow. He stopped growing not long after he passed the five-foot mark, so everyone eternally viewed him as a kid.

People in town seemed to go out of their way to look out for him. Some of that is just the way things are in a small west river town. Most of it was the love Coop drew to him the way butterflies flit around the brightest blossoms.

As we ate, my father swirled sugar into his cup, and

the spoon chimed against the cup like a boxing match bell. "You think Woof can take him?" he asked.

"Who?"

"Butch."

See, that's how it is in a small town. Folks know *everything* within minutes, and if they're parents, they know it *before* it happens. I didn't bother to ask how he knew what had happened before I even got there. Later, I learned they were taking odds down at the elevator. The odds were 10–1.

"Woof might be able to outrun him," I said.

"Might be the best tactic. Another thing. The guys at the elevator tell me Spook is back."

Coop stiffened.

I nodded.

Dad looked at Coop and me.

"You guys steer clear," he said. "Understood?"

The message was intended for Coop.

"Yes, sir," we said in unison.

After lunch, Mom gave me leftovers for my barren refrigerator. I rented an attic apartment in town. Technically, I lived there, but the rent money was largely wasted considering the time I spent at home.

"Will you do something for me?" she asked, not waiting for an answer. "I'm making a casserole. I want you to take it up to the Schwartzes later."

"Sure."

"How is Rose?"

"It's worse. Woof won't say so, but it's worse."

"Well, maybe she'll bounce back."

"Yeah. Well. Maybe."

"And Ella Peterson would like Coop to mow her lawn," Mom continued. "The grass ought to be dry enough by now. Do you have time to get him started before you go to work?"

Coop, who had a long list of yard work customers, really didn't need my help mowing, but she worried, and I did, too. Sometimes details escaped Coop.

There was the time when Marty Leesburg was up at the station getting spark plugs for his Ford Ranchero and Coop mowed right over a set of wrenches, sending a 9/16 Craftsman—*with a lifetime guarantee*—through the picture window, and the rest of the set pinging off the side of the faded pink trailer house where Marty's English war bride of thirty years was dozing. Sarah, in her lilting London accent, now oddly contaminated with cowboy twang, said it reminded her of the "fookin' blitz."

I agreed to help Coop.

"And, there's one more thing." My mother tucked a stray wisp of her black hair behind her ear. "It's Charlie Brown. It's worse. He can't make the stairs anymore. And when Coop carries him out to do his business, he yelps. It has to hurt pretty bad. You know, Charlie Brown never even complained when he got caught in that coyote trap."

Charlie Brown was supposed to be my dog, but Charlie never caught on. From the very first day, he latched onto Coop and Coop to him. I was allowed to borrow Charlie in the fall for pheasant hunting because after all, Charlie was a purebred Brittany. Charlie was a much better hunter than I was. I never was much of a shot, so each autumn I left the west river sky well ventilated, and most of the birds unscathed. Charlie would stare back at me with a look of disgust when I missed.

"What did they say down at the vet clinic?" I asked my mother.

"Norm says it's a tumor. He says even if he operated, Charlie probably wouldn't make it. He's seventeen, now. You know this can't go on."

I knew what that meant. "Does Coop know?"

"He's sure that if he prays enough, God will fix Charlie. He's been praying a lot."

"Okay, I'll handle it. But I'm going to take Charlie down to Joe Big Cloud tonight. Maybe he can do something."

"I thought you might. There's a rhubarb upside-down cake cooling on the rack. You take that down to Joe."

As good a veterinarian as Norm was, every rancher in the county knew of Joe's history of salvaging lost causes. If Joe had taken every case, he would have run Norm clean out of business, but he didn't. Eventually, folks figured out that Joe would politely decline to heal a steer, only to see it shipped to a Kansas feedlot and then to slaughter.

I think it was a matter of fairness. I don't think Joe thought it was right to give an animal hope, only to snatch it back a few weeks later. But a treasured cattle dog or a gifted quarter horse that had shared a score of roundups with a creaky old rancher—those were causes of merit. The sage would be lit, herbs gathered, and prayers prayed.

With the buzz of Coop's mower fading, I walked to the Farmers Union gas station. While I picked up a few bucks each week as a stringer for the *Pale Butte Sentinel*, the gas station was my full-time job. It wasn't glamorous, but it had its perks.

Marv let us play the radio. Between tires and oil changes we would tell jokes and lies and if it wasn't suffocatingly hot and the tune was right, Irv might dance. Long, lanky Irv would bounce and strut, arms flapping, with a grease rag dangling from his back pocket like an albatross bumbling through takeoff. *Play That Funky Music, White Boy!* I always thought that half the reason the gas station did such good business was the entertainment in the back.

Of course, there was Martha J. Wilcox. *She* didn't hurt business any. The fact is she kept the local chiropractor in business from all the neck cranking that took place when she walked from the bookkeeping office through the lobby. Even now, my chest feels like grapefruits are trying to work their way through the ventricles at the mention of her name. She was something, all right.

Martha was inventorying tires along the back wall when I walked in. She looked up from her clipboard, through her blond bangs, and smiled. As usual, my blood pressure soared, and my I.Q. plummeted to single digits.

"Hey, Bones, you aren't going to drop an Edsel off the hoist today, are you?"

My face flushed. "Naw. Gotta cut back. Big Edsel short-age. Haven't you heard?"

Her smile widened to reveal her teeth, perfect except for one slightly crooked incisor, which gave her smile a mischievous quality. She sashayed back to the lobby, giving me a little extra hip action because she knew I was staring.

Now, before we go any further and you start making assumptions that I'm some sort of incompetent, let me explain that the "Edsel Incident" wasn't really my fault. You see, for an oil change each car was lifted by a pair of cylinders—one for the front and one for the rear axle. One day, I was changing the oil in Ernie Larson's immaculate gunmetal gray '59 Edsel when the seal on the back cylinder of the hoist let loose, and the rear of the car started sliding off the rack. I sprinted for the lever to lower the front cylinder, but I couldn't get the nose down as fast as the rear was going. With the front end still four feet up, the car slipped off the rack, and the rear bumper banged the concrete with a hell of a racket. The front end bounced a good three feet up like a dribbled basketball.

The rear bumper was scuffed and smashed and the trunk was wrinkled like a cotton suit, but the front end was fine. It had impressive suspension. You have to give Ford that much. Marv was pretty mad, though—at least until he figured out the hoist was the problem, and that I could have easily been under the Edsel when it fell. Typically, he yelled first and asked questions later.

"Son of a bitch, Bones! Holy shit. Dammit, piss, shit!

Don't you know we don't fly the fuckin' cars off the rack! It ain't got wings! That's a fuckin' Edsel! It ain't goddamn Chitty Chitty Bang Bang!"

Ernie Larson was even madder. And considerably more profane.

Word spread quickly and some guys abandoned their breakfast at the café just to gawk and give me shit. After half the town had come over to look, Irv leaned across the tire cage with a grape Nesbitt's dripping sweat in his hand. "You know, Bones," he said. "If a fella's gonna drop a car from the ceiling, I figure it oughta be an Edsel. I ain't sure if it's ironic or poetic, but it's fitting."

A HEALING

When I think of Joe Big Cloud these days, I imagine him beside the river, calm and flat with the water reflecting the images of the pines on the opposite shore, disrupted only by the skittering of water bugs, the exuberant splash of a northern pike or the prehistoric beak of the snapping turtle with a shell the size of a '64 Chevy hubcap, rising to examine the world.

I wonder where Joe has gone—if he is in this world or that, in this dimension or another. Sometimes, he seems less real today after all these years. His lessons still test credulity. I start to explain away the happenings as coincidence and figments of delightful imagination. But that is the mind where he exists like a ghost, fleeting and fuzzy. It is in my heart where he lives and breathes and sings the shaman's song. It is my heart he taught me to trust.

I remember that the evening sun was still strong in the west but low enough that the beams of light had begun to glow in oranges and purples and pinks through the stratus, and I wonder now if we had never seen a sunset, if an artist's hand rendered it in oils for us in our caves of ignorance, would we believe such a thing could exist? Or would we dismiss it like Plato's Atlantis, like the canals on Mars?

People have always doubted, Missourians, all of us. Show us, or we cannot believe. We ignore what we feel. We discount the sage voices from within, the voice where the ethereal stations are fine-tuned. Instead we listen to the fuzzy distant radio waves of logic fading in and out.

I hear the scientists. I read the new theories only to see them smashed and dashed and ridiculed in years to come by fresh theories. I understand them not.

This is how it has been. We look back at the centuries, and we laugh at the notions—at the things they believed. Now, we sit in smug assurance that we, at long last, have processed the truth. Surely generations hence will not giggle at *us*.

How logical can logic be, I wonder, if it can see such sunsets as I have seen and not know there is a presence divine? We perceive the atoms and protons and neutrons and the subatomic, the matter and antimatter, so clearly. But the assemblage of the contraption we cannot fathom.

So I know as I tell of that summer with Joe Big Cloud and of the sunsets and of the things to come, some of you will doubt that it happened because you have not seen. I am not insulted. Doubt is healthy. It moves us forward, keeps us searching for truths, and repels stagnation. Doubt is uncomfortable, and discomfort moves us along and improves us here in this classroom. You may doubt, but when you open your mind you will see the truth. When you open your heart you will feel it. Open your soul and the light of mystic sunsets and sunrises shines in. It may happen today or in lifetimes to come.

But it will happen.

I wheeled Charlie Brown down to the river in Coop's Radio Flyer wagon. It was rusty brown, the red paint mostly a rumor. Coop used it to tote bags of leaves in the fall, and he tossed inside the weeds he plucked—and peas and corn and bean sprouts, too, before he learned to tell the difference. That day it was lined with Coop's good winter parka. He had insisted I use it when I explained I was going to take Charlie Brown for a walk. "Coop, Mom would have a conniption fit if she found out."

He raised his index finger to his lips to hush me. "Bones, can I come along?"

"Didn't you promise Mom you were going to help do the dishes?"

"Oh yeah."

I tried to make it a gentle ride, but even through the padding, the bumps elicited moans from the shallow-breathing Brit. It didn't look like Charlie Brown had much time.

Joe Big Cloud's bobber floated serenely on the north side of the dam. He sat on the flat angled boulder, still as the water, legs crossed underneath him. He was remarkably flexible for an older man, handsome, almost regal. He had black piercing eyes and a prominent but not overly large nose. His brown skin was still tight. His hair was black with just a few strands of gray at the temple. One long braid fell below his shoulder blades. Once and only once four greasers decided Joe needed a haircut. No one saw exactly what happened, but the four bleeding combatants were last seen wheeling out of town as fast their old Ford could go, and no one ever tested Joe again.

Joe did not turn when he heard the rattle of the wagon behind him, though you would have to be deaf not to hear it. He did not turn when I stepped down the short embankment and sat beside him.

I set Mom's cake in front of him like an offering before a prairie Buddha. His nostrils flared as he sniffed the caramel and rhubarb, the sweetness dancing and darting between the must and the rot of dead vegetation and beached bullheads along the shore. Now, I had his attention.

When I dropped my jaw to speak, he cocked his head to me.

"Joe, got a sick dog . . ."

He rotated his head to face me head-on, his eyes searching mine.

"Norm says it's a tumor."

He rose gracefully from his cross-legged position. In three quick steps he was up the embankment. Joe leaned over. Charlie Brown's eyes followed him, but his head remained down, resting on speckled front paws. Joe studied him for a long time.

"That's an old dog."

I agreed it was.

Joe contemplated some more as he looked into Charlie's eyes, and Charlie looked back into his. "It's his time," Joe said finally. "Time comes for us all." He scratched Charlie's ears.

I hung my head and softly pleaded Charlie's case. And Coop's. "Joe, I know it would be best to put him down. I know that. But I don't know if Coop is ready. I mean, if we could just have some more time to get him used to the idea of losing Charlie Brown. Maybe just a little more time."

"Leave him with me," Joe said finally after another interminable pause. "I have to think on it. And Charlie's got to think on it, too."

When I returned, Mom and Dad and I prepared Coop for the worst, and he listened politely. But he would not be dissuaded from his faith. Loss had not touched him yet. It spares youth, so we remember the early days fondly. But loss is inevitable, we told him. "I know," he said patiently with a pitying look as if *we* were the ones who were slow. "But I prayed, and Charlie Brown is coming home."

He did, too. Five days later, when Mom was sitting under the massive elm in our front yard, stitching a quilt, she looked up to see Charlie Brown walking slowly, purposefully toward the house. She rushed to the back porch where Coop was whittling. She stepped through the flaps and slivers of wood, atypically ignoring the mess.

"Coop, Charlie Brown is coming home!"

"I know," Coop said. "I prayed." Then he dropped his jackknife and bounded out to meet his dog.

One Saturday morning not long after that, Charlie Brown trotted along as Coop and I fetched the mail from the post office at the end of Main Street. We bumped into Norm coming through the glass door. He stopped short when he saw Charlie Brown bouncing along like a weaned pup. Charlie wagged his abbreviated tail. On his good days his wags consisted of a rapid wiggle of his hips from side to side. It was a good day and a great wag. Norm gently felt the abdomen where the tumor had been.

"Joe?"

"Yeah," I said.

Norm, who was always seemingly rushing from one barnyard crisis to another, took a moment to appreciate the miracle. He rubbed Charlie's neck. Charlie sat blissfully still for the massage. Norm stared down the street toward the river, as if he could see Joe through the thick growth of oaks and maples. And from beneath his perfectly waxed handlebar moustache, he smiled.

After Charlie's recovery, I gravitated more to Joe and the river. Coop wandered down almost daily, too, almost always bearing a gift—a particularly unusual stone or an exceptional blossom from Mom's bragging-rights flowerbed. If she spotted the larcenies, she did not protest, as she would have in any other summer.

Joe accepted each gift with reverence—including the

pies and cookies Mom passed along almost weekly. The non-perishable treasures from Coop were placed on the window-sill in the courthouse basement apartment where Joe had lived for more than thirty years. Mayor Bull Malone had set Joe up with the apartment and lifetime employment as the city handyman, because Bull owed him one.

Bull had been mayor since sometime around the end of the Stone Age despite his long-standing tradition of announcing his retirement at the end of each term. But each election write-in votes for Bull would sweep him in again. He would complain and bluster a bit as he held court in the café or at the Mecca Bar.

"You know, one of you boys is gonna have to step up to the plate next election."

They would all agree and not a one of them meant it, which really got Bull going. "I'm not foolin,' boys. Dammit to hell, I done my duty. And you guys sit here twiddlin' your thumbs . . . Buncha . . . thumb twiddlers!"

But after each election, he walked with his back a little straighter, paunch sucked in a bit tighter, and the plumes of smoke from his White Owl cigars billowed larger. He was a good king but tough, stubborn, and demanding, which meant the roads were cleared of snow in the winter and water main breaks fixed in short order even if it meant Bull had to climb down in the pit himself to help.

Bull was president of the Third National Bank of Pale Butte. He had a reputation for being cantankerous, but he would have walked through walls for Joe. Like I said, Bull owed him one. The debt was incurred before I was born, but the story was a matter of Pale Butte history. The details varied a little with each telling, but all agreed on a few points. No one had ever laid eyes on Joe until the day he pulled Bull's daredevil son, Astor, from the churning floodwaters of the Sneaky River.

That was one hell of a flood, they say. Only once since—in 1966—has a spring flood rivaled that one. I witnessed the flood in '66, and if the flood of 1947 was anything like that, it must have been something.

In '66 heavy snowfall and a swift melt up north sent a torrent rushing downstream overnight. They evacuated houses two blocks from the river. I thought it was folly. I could not imagine water rising that high, but by morning, water was lapping at the doors of those houses. Water thundered *over* the bridge. Normally, there was a twenty-foot drop.

Lefty Schlosser's old man opened the doors to his barn at the edge of town and the water washed through cleaning the stalls. It was the cleanest barn in the state until the waters receded, and the flood of spring lambs and calves washed back in on beds of straw.

Back in 1947, when he was seventeen and invincible as all of us are at that age, Astor Malone stared down from the steep hill above the river. If you have not seen such a thing, you can scarcely imagine the deafening rumble of the water, the way it makes the earth tremble. Take an immense prairie tornado, lay it on its side, fill it with froth, and that is what you will see. The ground shakes as if the earth is throwing a tantrum.

Astor Malone was legend back then for defiance of convention, for stretching the rules so far some blamed him for his father's baldness.

When he was nine, Astor fired up a Curtiss Jenny trainer, and if he had gotten the flaps right, he would have launched it off the dirt runway—and then he really would have had a problem. As it was, he took out a barbwire fence bordering the landing strip and flipped the plane.

When he was fifteen, he leaped from the water tower, a hundred twenty-five feet up, with an army surplus parachute. He would have been killed if the billowing chute hadn't caused him to drift just enough to snag the springy branches of a towering elm tree as he plummeted, leaving him hanging fifty feet from disaster as if crucified, bloodied and scraped raw by tree bark but alive. Very much alive.

As he watched the fury of the water, Astor told Muck Kendall, "I'm going to swim it," and with the roaring of the water in his ears, Muck didn't understand what he had said until Astor jumped into the maelstrom.

I have considered Astor's decision often, trying to understand. I don't think Astor believed he would die. It was exhilaration he sought. But if you think about it, if you could hold off the fear, dying that way would be quite a ride. One wild ride.

When Astor went under, washing under the bridge, Muck lost sight of him. But finally Astor appeared two hundred yards downstream, unconscious or dead. His body was rammed up against the branches of a massive oak wedged tenuously between the dirt embankments. The bank was washing away by the second, so Muck knew it wouldn't be long before the tree and Astor would be washed downstream. But Astor's limp body was thirty yards away from the west bank with the hellish grinding, churning between. His head was barely above water. Muck went for help, crawling across the shuddering top girders of the bridge and then sloshing up to Main Street.

Grumpy Mindeman was the first one there, hauling a loop of rope, he told me in a sober moment during his monthly dry time when his veteran's pension check had run out. "I had no idea how I was going to get the rope to Astor and with him unconscious or dead, how was he going to grab it?" he said. But when Grumpy and Muck arrived, and fifty others followed to watch Astor die, the oak had washed another hundred yards farther downstream. They were too late.

Then someone spotted the body of Astor Malone lying high on the hill overlooking the river. Leaning over him was a stranger.

Grumpy says Bull Malone wept that day on that hill. Rushing from his desk, he ran knowing he had lost his only son. But we sprint to sorrow sometimes in this life. Bull ran, and miraculously found his son returned, coughing and spitting and shivering beside a young Lakota man. Bull embraced his son, kneeling on the buffalo grass, looking up in wonder at this new friend.

Some said Joe Big Cloud had ridden the rails of the Milwaukee Road Railroad boxcars to town like a thousand hard-luck bums who came through town in those days. Joe never said. I wonder if angels ride the rails, if medicine men huddle in the echoes and urine stench of empty boxcars.

I wonder.

"We never did figure out how Joe pulled him out without a rope," Grumpy told me as we sat on the bench across from the Mecca Bar, warming in the sun. He rolled his last cigarette with trembling hands. The empty red Prince Albert can clanged against the garbage barrel beside the bench. He lit his cigarette and drew deeply.

"Even if he had a rope, there wasn't a damn thing to tie it to." He puffed again, and the shaking subsided. He looked down at the swirls of dust around his ankles and then at me, gray eyes clear.

"Funny thing, though. Astor was soaked through and through, and his lips were blue. We had to strip off his clothes and cover him with jackets. 'Cuz of hypothermia."

He took a long drag, expelled it, and leaned closer.

"The funny thing is, Joe Big Cloud was dry as a bone."

THE TURTLE

Mayor Bull Malone saw to it that Joe's duties were eased as the years collected. It's not that Joe couldn't have kept doing the hard jobs—it's just that Bull didn't think he should have to. So, Joe fished most mornings before the shrouds of mist lifted and the grays slowly came alive with color. He might fish again in the evening after he had groomed the graves at the city cemetery that overlooked his fishing spot.

That summer Bull hired Coop to mow the park below the cemetery. It was a beautiful park, a comforting place to sit, where gnarled trees leaned gently over to the river.

One day, Coop stopped mowing by the stone arch entrance to the park when he saw a car brake hard and swerve around what turned out to be the moss-covered, drying shell of the giant old snapping turtle we often saw sunning himself on the dam. Now, he was traversing the softening tar of the road on some mysterious pilgrimage.

Fearing the next vehicle would kill the snapper, Coop came to the rescue. When he got there, the old snapper ducked his massive blunt head inside the shell. His powerful, stubby clawed feet sucked up inside, too. Coop struggled to lift the monster, which might have been pushing seventy pounds or more, but when the turtle felt himself airborne for the first time in fifty years, he kicked Coop's hand loose. The snapper fell and landed on the dome of his shell. When Coop began to right him, the powerful beak clamped down hard on his wrist, breaking skin and cracking bone.

Coop screamed as he dragged the turtle to safety. There, in the tall grass of the ditch, the assailant abandoned the grip in favor of escape, still hissing prehistorically. Holding his bleeding limb, Coop sought Joe, who was tending to a fresh grave.

Tearing the tail from Coop's shirt, Joe bound the wound as Coop complained bitterly about the unfairness of it all. There, among the stunted granite and marble monoliths, Joe soothed him before sending him on his way home.

"I was just trying to help the turtle," Coop explained as Dad examined the wound on the front steps before supper. It was bad, but the torn flap of skin had been bound in place expertly and it was already beginning to mend at such a pace Dad decided against stitches. These are the things we grew to expect from Joe Big Cloud.

"Joe says we don't always understand when someone's trying to help us," Coop said.

Dad thought about that for a moment, glancing up at me. "He's right."

"And he said sometimes when people act like they're helping you, they really aren't." My father nodded. "And he said I was *your* turtle."

Dad furrowed his brow. Coop did the same.

"Well, sometimes your head's as hard as a turtle's shell. . . ." My father rapped his knuckles gently on Coop's noggin. Coop squirmed and smiled at the teasing. And then Dad rose, steering Coop inside.

Many years later, I finally sorted out what Joe had meant. It was in my father's final year, though we didn't know it then. Dad and I were speaking about old friends and of times past and, of course, of Joe Big Cloud. We laughed as we remembered the attack of the snapping turtle. When the guffaws had dwindled to chuckles and then to silence, I recalled the cryptic sentence.

"Dad, I think I know why Coop was the turtle."

Dad leaned forward in his chair. He was shrunken by the years, but his eyes were still sharp. They became distant as he remembered that summer.

Most of us surrounding Coop had been willing to coddle him because of his disability. When frustration set in at the confusing loops, we tied his shoes for him as my father snorted in disgust. We babied him. And Coop was not above playing on our sympathies.

Every fall, after the first frost, my father would back the elevator's smoke-belching green 1959 Chevy Apache pickup into the yard so the season's first load of coal could be shoveled into the bin. It had always been my job.

"Coop!" my father demanded one fall day. Coop slowly extracted himself from the television screen and meandered to the kitchen. "Coop, I want you to get the grain scoop out of the basement and shovel the coal into the bin."

When Coop began to complain, my father cut him off. "Move it!"

"He's just a boy," my mother said, as Coop jumped to the task.

"He's getting soft!"

"You can't expect—"

"You expect too little," he interrupted, biting off the words.

"But things are harder for him."

"Then he needs to work harder. Olivia, you will not always be here to fend for him and neither will I."

"Bones will be here."

"Bones needs to have a life of his own."

So my father demanded. He cajoled. And in time, Coop delivered. And my mother and I accepted, privately, at least, that Dad had been right. For years, though, Coop grumbled behind my father's back as he completed his chores, snapping protests vitriolic, as my father carried him unappreciated to safer ground.

"That is why Coop was the turtle," I said.

My father leaned back under the blanket. His eyes glistened. "I know," he said softly.

AND THEN THERE WERE THREE

It is amazing to be loved. And to be loved by someone amazing is, well, amazing. It was a Sunday morning when Venus arrived in Pale Butte and stole our hearts, never returning them.

Woof and I were red-eyed at the time after bongs for breakfast at Mutt's place where incense burned and black lights flickered. As we smoked, church bells chimed invitations to another meditation, ringing in time and then out of time with Pink Floyd on eight-track.

It was a curious neighborhood.

To the west of Mutt's place was the parsonage, the current address of the Reverend Lomas K. Brown, who sweated on such summer mornings from the pulpit of St. Andrew's Lutheran Church.

To the east was the tidy two-bedroom home of Martha J. Wilcox, widowed by a Vietnam sergeant who had experienced the vast extremes of fortune, first by marrying Martha with curves like Daytona and a voice smokier than Mutt's living room at midnight, and then by managing to be the last official casualty in Vietnam.

Dayton Wilcox met Martha just ten minutes after buying into the recruiter's vision of the glories of war. He was just ten minutes—*six hundred seconds*—from a perfect life. Instead, ninety-two days, six hours, and thirteen minutes from an honorable discharge, the poor bastard falls out of a helicopter lifting off from a Saigon rooftop.

I ponder the ironies of such things. From above, this big beautiful blue machine appears to float and revolve in blackness and silence, but down here, gears clatter and click seemingly in need of grease, and another irritating red stoplight is one car's savior while the station wagon that made the light is obliterated two blocks down the road by a speeding Peterbilt. Meanwhile, oblivious to the divine providence that has saved them, the ones at the red light curse their perceived misfortune.

So some live, propagate, the family name marches on, and up ahead amidst the smoke, the broken glass, the weeping, the regrets, and flashing red lights, generations vanish unborn.

I marvel at the way things string together, the way everyday moments bring us crashing together or veering apart. And all the while we are in the passenger seat we believe we are driving.

Six hundred seconds steered Martha here from St. Paul to these buttes and red scoria roads and the home Dayton's parents had passed to him and from him to her. That was what we had learned of the beautiful stranger in the three years she had lived in Pale Butte. That, and one other detail . . . It was common knowledge she had killed a man.

Herman Boschee was a gardener. I think the reason old folks dig in the dirt so much is so they can get comfortable with it, because they're going to be there soon. Anyway, after Martha moved in next door, Herman developed a serious obsession with the six-foot hedge separating the properties. That Martha spent her lunch hours basting and overflowing from the modest constraints of a bikini in the backyard is probably a coincidence, but in the interest of thoroughness, I mention it.

Herman started eating less at noon, declining seconds of perfectly good German food prepared by his wife, Ione, so maybe malnutrition had something to do with it. It might have been sheer exhaustion. By August, the Boschee backyard was immaculate. Every dandelion had been banished, not a blade of grass jutted unmanicured, and the hedge was down to four feet. Of course, Ione knew what was going on, but there had been an uncommon resurgence in the bedroom, and well, after fifty-three years of marriage, you don't argue the origin of blessings.

All I know is the very same day Martha rolled to her back, forgetting (that's what she said) to pull up the straps to her top, is the day Herman keeled over with pruning shears in his hand, seriously dead from his first and only heart attack.

After Ione headed across the border to a Boonesville

nursing home where they have bingo every Saturday, Mutt moved into the house, and the dandelions returned.

Six hundred seconds had transformed a neighborhood six hundred miles away.

So excuse me if I don't believe in coincidence. Not anymore. At the time, I didn't recognize the fine weave around me of lives looping together, fraying at the edges sometimes, but I glimpse it more often today, and when I meet the beautiful strangers, in the back of my mind as the pleasantries are exchanged, and we lament meteorological excesses, I wonder what gears have been set in motion and where it will lead.

I think about the pinballs bouncing.

Of course, I wasn't thinking about any of that the day my world changed. The girl who changed everything didn't bounce into my life as much as she glided in.

I saw the first glint of sunlight off the chrome fender of the ten-speed Schwinn as Woof and I shuffled down the side street. She was headed our way. She had strawberry hair, and long legs, tan and perfect. As she pedaled closer, steering to the right to pass, Woof stepped out suddenly in front of the bike, which braked to a halt. On his foot.

"Hold on there, missy. This here's a holdup!" he drawled. It was an abysmal John Wayne impersonation. The redhead looked at him, then at me, and I wished I had worn a better shirt. Her eyelids hovered low over green eyes.

"Let me guess," she said coolly, looking at Woof. "You're Moe and this must be Curly. Say, Moe, aren't you short a Stooge?"

"Actually, I'm . . . Simon," Woof blustered. "And this is Garfunkel. You mighta heard about us. We're pretty big around here."

"Pleased to meet you. I'm Toni Tennille. The Captain couldn't make it."

She was also known as Maya Swendsen, granddaughter of Gus and Bertha Martell. She was seventeen, destined for Stanford but abandoned for the summer while Mum and Daddy spent the summer in Europe away from his South Jersey plastics firm whose slick, shiny, and artificial products bore close resemblance to the marriage they were trying to mend.

Maya bounced the front tire hard on Woof's foot and when it retreated, she placed a white canvas boat shoe on the top pedal. My eyes followed the delicate ankle past the detour of her knee and upward until I could feel her eyes on me. Bedroom eyes still at half-staff, she looked at me. The corners of her mouth rose almost imperceptibly, but I recognized it for what it was, impossible as it might have seemed—a smile.

Her calf flexed as the pressure on the pedal built. "Garfunkel, I thought you were magnificent on *Bridge over Troubled Water*," she said. The bike lurched forward. I nervously picked at the dime-sized hole near the faded mystery stain on my theoretically white T-shirt.

"See yuh, Simple Simon," she called, not looking back, as the tic, tic, tic of the ten-speed faded to silence. Woof and I pivoted as if choreographed to watch her.

So it began, a connection of hearts, clunking and shuddering like the coal cars at the elevator coupling, solid and graceful just the same. She seemed wiser than I was though I was older, and the distance in sophistication between us was as great as the distance between Dakota and Jersey. I cannot forget the kisses, soft and tender, tongues dancing, even though since that time my heart has opened wide, shut down to mourn, and ventured open again.

Maya, Woof, and I became a gang of three with banter worthy of the Round Table at the Algonquin Hotel. Even Joe was not immune. We knocked on his door when the gas tank was dry or Woof had dropped the clutch or another rear end out of his sunshine yellow '63 four-door Impala.

It was our holy place. Our din would hush in respect for Joe Big Cloud and for the songs of Lady Day, Dinah Washington, and Peggy Lee drifting from the speakers powered by an old Dynaco ST-70 tube amplifier that made everything sound lush and romantic.

Maya loved the jazz, Gilbert and Sullivan, and the Gershwins. She would sit with Joe, perfectly centered between the speakers to hear the rising thump of the bass, building a platform for Ella Fitzgerald and the rhythm that pit-a-pats through her brain.

Meanwhile, Woof and I pondered the advances and retreats of knights, bishops, and pawns from the white enamel table trimmed in red above firm chromed legs.

The nights were ours.

In daylight that summer, Woof paid his dues in leather gloves, stretching barbwire at the Lazy J Ranch, replacing miles of old fence to make way for a new blacktop to the west. It was wider, so the fence had to be moved back a hundred feet.

I raised pickups and cars on the hoist to change oil, filled gas at the pump, and watched Irv invent terrible new dance steps.

Maya laughed at Grandpa Gus' stories each time they were told, and when Grandma Bertha wasn't looking, Maya scrubbed deeper into the crannies proud myopic grandmothers begin to miss.

ENTER THE COWBOY

Twice when gladiators have met, I have feared for the outcome. In 1974, I was miserable waiting for the radio reports from Kinshasa, wondering which round would be the one George Foreman caught up to an aging Ali and killed him. In 1971, I had mourned the loss to Frazier after Ali's return to the ring, and now I was ready to do it again.

But the carnival hucksters have their days. If I held no hope for Ali in '74, I had considerably less for Woof when Butch finally cornered him.

There was something about the buttes to the northwest that produced the meanest, toughest sons of bitches you'll ever see. On weekends, they rolled off ranches ornery and thirsty, just itching for a fight. When the invaders came, we steered clear, humored them, and held our breath until closing time at the Mecca Bar.

It was a rare weekend that fists didn't fly. Bob's wife, Bernice, kept a fungo bat under the bar. If she was taller than five feet, it was only by the grace of her jet-black beehive hair.

"The higher the hair, the closer to God," she said. But when the trouble started, she was no one to trifle with. You'd find her in the middle of it, beating bodies like an Alaska musher breaking up a dogfight in the traces.

Those with the courage to stand up to Butch were summarily and brutally dispatched, sometimes before Bernice even got there. But worse was the fate of those who cowered. About the worst thing you could be was a gutless wonder—*a chickenshit.* But after you took the beating, which was a foregone conclusion, there was some respect to be salvaged—assuming you lived.

That was our dumb-ass code. You didn't run from a fight. Hell, you ran to it!

Anyway, I was on my way to my fourth straight win over Woof on the pool table in the back, which was some kind of record, and Butch watched from the bench along the wall gulping beers and waiting his turn on the other table. That he had been hustled by a smart ass that apparently wasn't even good enough to beat *me* must have added to his irritation, I think. Woof ignored the stares. Or tried to.

When Butch's turn came on the other table, he walked over to Woof. "That's my cue," he said. The truth is, it was a three-dollar bar cue indistinguishable from all the others hanging on the rack. Woof turned and swallowed hard. Time stopped, and everyone stared. They'd seen this dance before.

"Butch, there's lots of cues in the rack," Woof said politely, as if the matter was at all negotiable.

"That's *my* cue," Butch insisted. He clenched his fist.

"Look," Woof said, "I'm not . . ."

Butch stepped closer. "You stupid or hard of hearing?"

"Both!" I answered for Woof. "C'mon, Woof," I urged. "Give him the goddamn cue."

And Woof did. It came whistling around butt end first and caught him right across his ear. Butch went down hard, bleeding from his split right ear, and a lesser man would have stayed there. The lobe was dangling by a hunk of skin. Woof looked at me with wide eyes. His hands still clutched the broken stub of the cue. When Butch started to get up, Woof's eyes got wider still. Because if Butch got to his feet Woof was surely going down. So he tackled the monster and latched onto his neck. Still the big man rose with Woof cranking like a defiant, doomed kitten on the neck of a German shepherd.

Butch began lurching around, trying to loosen Woof's grip, and when that didn't work, he began battering Woof's body into the wall and then into the pool table like an enraged Brahma bull. Tables were upended, and Norm was sent skidding on his ass, beer in hand, across the floor when his chair was kicked from underneath him. To his credit, he did not spill a drop.

Each time he was bashed against the wall, Woof grunted, and spittle and blood flew from his mouth. Then Butch began hammering on Woof's head, thunderous, looping punches over the grip around his neck, raising welts with massive knuckles. By that time, Bernice had the fungo bat out and was swinging like Roger Maris in '61, and Woof was getting the worst of it. "Dammit, Bernice," he yelled, "what are you hitting me for? I'm the one getting the shit kicked out of me!"

"Then take your beating like a man, and quit wrecking the joint!"

But almost imperceptibly, Butch's hammer blows weakened as his air supply was cut off. And then it became obvious that he was fading. Woof hung on as Butch struggled, now on the floor, legs splayed out, his thick neck caught tight in the vise of Woof's elbow.

"Tell me you're done, and I'll let go," Woof whispered into the bloody ear.

Butch heaved in a final effort to escape. No good.

"Tell me you're done, Butch. *Or I gotta kill you,*" Woof hissed. I think he meant it, too, because if Butch got loose, Woof was certainly a dead man. There was a pause—a very long pause.

"I'm done," Butch finally croaked.

Woof let go and rose unsteadily to his feet. Bernice stood by, her club at the ready. Wheezing, Butch sprang to his feet like a jungle cat and glared at Woof, his barrel chest heaving, and for a moment I thought he was going to reengage. Both of them were bloody. Woof's head was lumpy with welts. One eye was puffy. With the exception of his ear, Butch looked all right.

I know Woof was surprised to still be alive—*at least at being conscious*—but the need for diplomacy did not escape him. "Buy you a beer?" he offered. As if Butch needed another. Butch shrugged, and the observers parted like the Red Sea to make way.

They sat for the longest time without speaking. Woof held a frosted mug of Grain Belt beer against the knots on his forehead. Butch winced now and then as Norm stitched the dangling earlobe with heavy black sutures retrieved from his veterinary truck parked out front.

When his lungs had settled down to a normal cadence, Butch cocked his head to Woof, studying him curiously for a moment, looking at him like you might, fruitlessly, into a window opaque with frost. You know there's something going on inside. You witness fleeting shadows. You just can't make it out.

"You know I can take you, don't you?" Butch said finally.

Woof stared straight ahead. He started to grin, but it hurt, so he stopped.

"Yeah," he said.

And so Butch entered our lives, bashing down the door, completing our Gang of Four, providing the fourth direction.

To the north, where blizzards sweep with no conscience, Woof, the pragmatist, stands, dueling with the pelting snow, reeling sometimes from the wind, slipping away before the force can pull him down. He feints. He bobs. He weaves on the edge.

Me? I stand in the east where the hope of a new day rises. I savor the fresh beginnings, and the prospect of the day's perfection, and when the Edsels come crashing down, I shrug and wait for the newer day.

And Maya . . . She is in the comfortable south, source of warm breezes, genteel smiles, and sassy kisses. She lives in the easy home of fond memories, waving slyly from the stoop.

Butch roams the west because it is where the cowboys go. Pushing, pulling, sweating, grunting, racing to beat the day, pausing at dusk to appreciate the victorious sun as it settles past the finish-line horizon of those flat-topped buttes.

The taciturn Butch would sigh sometimes at the chatter in Woof's Impala as we cruised at thirty-five miles per hour on desolate back roads. He rode shotgun, slipping Marshall Tucker into the eight-track when we weren't watching. It was as close to cowboy music as Woof carried in his collection.

Woof would pilot, sliding from second gear to third and back again with the Hurst shifter. The 327-cubic-inch motor would pop the Cherry Bomb mufflers, which weren't really mufflers at all. It was a glorious sound—the sound of being young.

In the backseat, Maya and I sat stealing kisses when we were willing to endure the sophomoric complaints and heckling about the romance from up front. Butch would lean close over the console, and Woof would throw his arm passionately around him, both making smacking noises.

"Oh, you are muh big strong man." Butch swooned like Scarlett O'Hara.

"Now gimme a little sugar," Woof demanded, pursing his lips.

We watched the act, bemused, from the backseat.

"I believe I liked it better when they weren't friends," I said.

"But they do make a cute couple," Maya said.

I had begun to miss her already.

It is rare to have someone burst into your life and envelop you the way she did. It seems to me that some folks spend dry, banal, tentative lives together while others manage to wedge a lifetime's depth into a few profound weeks. I had fallen instantly and irrevocably in love with her. Everyone had. Woof was clearly taken with her. She even managed to make old stone face Joe smile—grin, even—during our frequent visits.

I mourned the scarcity of minutes between the two of us and Stanford, and my heart ached from missing her even as I draped my arm around her and she squirmed in close. I began to plot ways to follow her to California, desperate, impossible schemes hatched, never shared, and regretfully abandoned. I had never mourned the living before, mourned the loss even as I held her tight.

These days, even as my eyes squint to read the road signs bulleting past, my heart sees clear and distant, and I know even as I am blessed with the years, I am cursed with the coming loss of those I love, dropping unexpectedly like flies.

Dancing into my life. Lurching away without good-byes.

So each day I mourn. And each day they are with me, I celebrate.

Perspective is mine, but little else can I claim in permanence.

One midweek day that June, I was mourning the losses to come when I found myself at the river's edge. Maya had been claimed for the day by her grandmother's family picnic. An uncommonly brave meadowlark sat chirping on the boulder beside Joe but fluttered away when I arrived.

Joe listened to my lament as we gazed at the serene water. The turtle's nose poked up, watching, too, from the other bank.

"I love her," I blurted glumly somewhere in the conversation. "And now I am going to lose her."

He listened, impassive as always, measuring my words. Even though I did not speak aloud my jealousies, he saw the vison bouncing vile and sickly green in my mind. I saw nameless California college boys. Handsome, smart, and wealthy with flashy red sports cars, and the sons of bitches were taking Maya away from me.

"Ah, but to lose something, you must have first gained something," Joe said. He was silent as I approached my heartache from that perspective. When a moment had passed, he asked, "So where do you feel her?" He pointed first to his head and then to the center of his chest.

"In my heart," I answered.

"Good," he said. "When you live within your heart, no one is ever lost. Your friends are there. Coop is there. Your mother and father are there. They will never leave."

"It's just that I've never had anyone like her," I said. "I just wish there was some way to keep her here."

"Can you have her if her mind is elsewhere and if her spirit is not with you? You may hold on tight with your arms, but her spirit will go where it wishes. Is a bird in a cage really yours?" Joe looked at me, but I could only stare at my shoes. I know he was not trying to make me feel small. But I felt small, just the same.

When he had let the words settle in, he continued. "Many days the meadowlark comes to me to talk. And then he flies away. If he returns tomorrow, is that not a greater gift?"

I nodded.

"Maya must fly where the wind takes her. But you will always be able to visit her in your heart, and if she chooses, she will keep you in her heart, and across the miles your hearts will know, and they will speak even if you do not think you can hear the whispers. Maya is a bird. But she cannot soar if you hold her back."

Great.

Coop is a turtle.

And now Maya is a bird.

So what am I? Probably some kind of weasel.

"I'm still going to miss her," I said.

Joe looked at me and then across the bank where the lambs were settling in under the pines. One of them was dragging a hind leg.

"Me, too," he said.

SPOOK THE PREDATOR

Click. Click, click, click. That's how I spent my spare time—
hammering out a story a week as a stringer for the *Pale Butte
Sentinel*. Gunnar Smithers paid top dollar—twenty-five cents
a column inch—and I have to admit I looked for ways to
increase my paycheck. I could turn a story about Ella Peterson's turnip shaped like Millard Fillmore into a treatise on
the thirteenth president with a digression into the latest con-
cert at The Fillmore and how Led Zeppelin's blues couldn't
hold a candle to anything Joplin or Hendrix had done there
in the Sixties. You might have noticed. Sometimes I ramble.

Smithers calmly edited most of it out in the beginning. "Who's this Lem Zeppler and what does he have to do
with turnips?"

"Nothin,' I guess."

The blue pen would come out and the paragraph would
be struck.

"And what's *visceral* mean?"

I didn't know. Not exactly.

"We'll if you don't know what it means, I'm not payin' you for it. You know, son, this ain't exactly rocket surgery."

In the beginning, Smithers must have figured he wouldn't go broke, judging from the typing display I put on when he called me to see if I was fit for the job. He blanched as he watched me peck away with two fingers. "Nineteen words per minute," he said, clicking his stopwatch. "You won't be workin' on the Linotype anytime soon 'less we switch from a weekly to a monthly."

I hung my head.

"On the other hand, there aren't any typos." That was about as close to a compliment as Smithers ever gave me, and I think the only reason he gave me that much was because none of this was really my idea. My old English teacher, Mrs. Roland, put him up to it. I guess she didn't like me looking so *aimless*, so she called Smithers and told him I had written a few stories in high school composition that had been good enough to read out loud and that if someone didn't provide some direction in my life, I would end up in jail for sure.

Click. Click. Click.

Skip. Skip. Skip. There were footsteps keeping perfect time to the keys, and then the door flew open. It was still vibrating against the doorstop when Maya's lips met mine and we kissed hungrily. I nibbled her neck, but she seemed distracted. Abruptly, she pulled away and walked to the window, which looked two and a half stories down to the street.

"What is it?" I asked as I walked toward her.

"Oh, nothing. It's just . . . *Who is that?*" She pointed to a large figure skulking in the shadows of a weeping willow across the street. Spook.

Spook was a predator. As a lumbering child, with pale skin almost translucent, he pulled the wings and legs off box elder bugs for entertainment as if dismantling Tinkertoys. He put frogs in Mason jars and tossed them into the burning barrels in the alley. When he got older, neighborhood pets began to disappear. We buried my cat, Smokey, when I was eight, after she came home staggering from a dose of rat poison.

And then there was what he did to Coop. I never stopped feeling guilty about it. I was supposed to be his protector, but I had not been there when Coop wandered into Spook's yard and almost didn't make it back out. When he had him cornered, Spook picked up a scrap two-by-four about three feet long, and methodically beat Coop with the lumber from ankle to head like he was tenderizing a round steak.

Pop. Now the spider has seven legs.

Sizzle. The frog screams unheard, roasting in the Mason jar.

Groan. The cat gasps, eyes rolling, as arsenic gnaws through her guts.

Thud. Beat the lovely retarded boy.

Crack. Break those bones.

Smile. Listen to the whimpering.

Thud. He is loved and I am not.

Thud. Such a lovely day.

Thud.

Ella Peterson spotted Coop crawling on the edge of the blacktop three blocks from home that day and somehow dragged him into the Corvette and drove with the horn blaring right through our front yard, over the sidewalk, and to the front door. Coop fell out of the car and staggered up the steps, leaning on Ella. As badly as he was hurt, he moved with a sense of urgency as if something was chasing him. My mother and I almost collided at the door, rushing from opposite ends of the house.

His breath was ragged, and he was crying in desperate heaves.

"Baby, what happened to you?" my mother asked, her tone rising with each word before she caught herself and finished the sentence in measured tones. She reached to hug him but pulled back, unsure of where she could touch him without hurting him more.

Coop looked at her and then at me. It was a desperate look. And he wailed. "Spppoook!"

When I heard Spook's name, I grabbed my Nellie Fox Louisville Slugger while Mom dialed the town cop. Of course, by then Tiny already knew what had happened. Like I said, news travels fast in a small town.

I found Spook in the alley, a half block away from his home, but Woof had found him first. Tiny was there, too, leaning his three-hundred-pound bulk against his tan Rambler, watching as Woof worked Spook over.

Spook was on his face, trying to raise his bulk. But

each time he got to his knees, Woof kicked him again in the ribs with a sickening plop. As it went on, I started to get concerned, twisting the thick handle of the bat nervously the way I did when I crowded the plate against the fireballers. This was worse than anything Nellie Fox and I had imagined dishing out.

"Tiny, maybe you should stop it."

"Yup," he said, but remained immobile.

"Jesus, Tiny!"

Finally, four kicks later, he shifted and moved closer. "That's enough, Woof."

"Is he still breathing?" Woof asked.

"Looks like it," Tiny said.

"Then it ain't enough."

"I dunno, Woof. Murder means a lot of paperwork. You know I don't like paperwork. Everything in goddamn triplicate, these days. And you know I don't type worth shit. . . ."

With Spook once again flat on his face, Woof stomped hard with the heel of his black engineer boot on the back of Spook's right hand and then on his left, crunching both hands like brittle leaves underfoot in October. It would be a long time before Spook could pick up another club.

About that time Bertram Sumpter arrived from the blacksmith shop with his filthy shop coat on, sleeves straining from arms as solid as the iron he shaped on his anvil. Bertram was Tiny's official part-time deputy. There was nothing he liked better than someone who might be inclined to resist arrest. Bertram also served as jailer on the rare occasions someone actually ended up in jail. It was good the jail didn't get used much because prisoners had a lot of accidents around the holding cell.

"Tiny, you want I should throw the freak into the cop car?" Bertram asked.

Tiny cuffed Spook, and Bertram tossed him into the back of the Rambler, but not before slamming Spook's face into the door frame.

"Well, excuse me! Did I miss? Please accept my apology. Now git your freak ass in there and don't bleed all over the seat."

Woof pushed past me, breathing hard. I scurried to catch up. He was headed to my place to check on Coop.

"Woof, you didn't need to . . ."

"Goddamn right I did."

Coop was sitting on a stool by the sink, shirt off, as Mom cleaned up the ugly welts. He smiled at Woof through the lumps on his jaw as he held the ice pack over his right eye. A sliver of eyeball peeked through the swelling.

"Howya doin', Coop?" Woof's voice boomed with bravado, but his hands were trembling.

"Spook hurt me."

"I know, buddy," Woof said softly, leaning over to study the welts. "It won't happen again."

When Mom was done fixing what could be fixed, Woof carried Coop in his arms like a shepherd with a lost lamb to the couch where Coop stayed for three days until Mom tired of the filibuster and let him resume his neighborhood visitations, stiffly limping, smiling sweetly through chipped teeth, making sure to collect his ration of cookies at Ella's.

Woof visited every day Coop was laid up, watching *Lone Ranger* reruns with him after school, making him laugh so much, Coop complained his ribs hurt. With each visit and each kindness, Mom nodded in approval as her eyes snagged Woof's. Then they would both turn away to hide the tears.

"Best to keep your distance," I told Maya. I peered out the window again, but Spook had vanished. I sat back down and stared at my typewriter and stared hard at the lines on the paper.

"Whatcha writing?"

" 'Bout the fire. Smithers wants a story by tomorrow."

"Those poor people."

"Well, no one died."

"But they lost everything."

When Bertram Sumpter's house burned down, it was a sad moment to be sure. Olga Sumpter cried about the family photos lost to the fire, and I felt guilty about feeling so ambivalent about it. Maybe it's just the Dakota stoic in me, but if you need photos to stir the memories, then maybe the memories weren't that important in the first place.

I'm not saying it wasn't sad, but I looked around and saw Olga and Bertram—who was staggering around drunk—and three puzzled kids in nightshirts on the lawn, I saw it as a victory. There would be no caskets and dirges.

There was a dead cat lying curiously unsinged on the lawn, but beyond that, God help me, I didn't see tragedy. In my mind I could see a new house going up, clean and smelling of pine lumber. I saw a new beginning. I will mourn people, but I cannot bring myself to mourn *things*.

That's not how I wrote it, though. I wrote how it was all very sad, and what a close call it was, and how it was the first Pale Butte house lost in a fire since 1942, and how folks could send their contributions to St. Andrew's Lutheran Church if they wanted to help out.

Smithers nodded with approval and didn't change one single word.

IF NOT FOR THE HAUNTING

It could have been perfect. That summer could have been perfect if not for the premonitions that weighed heavy upon my shoulders like a wet wool blanket. I tried to brush them off, wish them away, discount it as imagination or worse, as buds of insanity, but like unwelcome distant relatives dropping in just as dinner is served, they returned, persistent and hungry.

I tried, but I could not keep any of this from Maya.

We were in the gazebo in the park studying the gouges I had carved a week before: *Maya and Bones Forever.* The carving had already begun to fade to the dull gray of a thousand other proclamations of love carved there and now forgotten or spoiled.

I was distant that day. Brooding.

"Are you okay?" she asked, touching my wrist.

"Fine."

Her eyes searched mine.

I tried to tell her what was on my mind, but what

could I tell her? I mean, there were tangible concerns. Like what was wrong with the Minnesota Twins this year? And what exactly was I planning to do with my life? Spend it dribbling Edsels off the concrete at the gas station, getting comfortable, never reaching, and then suddenly find myself another old hermit, picking at paint chips on the benches on Main Street, getting more loopy with the years? And what was I going to tell her about this specter I could feel hovering?

Sure, I'll just tell her I've got a bad feeling. Then I'll sound like the grumpy old farmers who predict a drought every year and worry more when it doesn't happen. Then I'll start predicting the weather based on the aches in my joints and spend my time boring the living shit out of anyone I can corner, with stories of the good old days when the crops were good and the blizzards were really something. Sure, that's what I'll tell her. And then I'll slit my wrists.

I couldn't tell her how I pictured her pulling away from the City Café waving from the window of a Jackrabbit bus. I couldn't begin to tell her how it made me feel.

Then there was Woof. I couldn't remember a time when I had ever worried about Wolfgang Harold Schwartz, but I was worried now. From the early days of our childhood I never considered Woof to be anything but impervious to the unpleasant things of life. But now, for the first time, in brief flickers amidst the usual bombast, I swear I could see uncertainty. Perhaps even vulnerability. My whole life Woof had been unshakable.

"Mom sent me over to the Schwartzes with a hot dish," I explained finally. "Woof wasn't back from the ranch . . . Tanya was out . . . Rose was at the table, writing a letter, I thought. She looked like she had been crying."

"About what?"

"That's what I wondered. When she put the pan into the oven, I could see what she was writing."

"And?" I could feel her eyes trying to lift mine. Finally Maya won, and I looked and then stared down again at the floorboards of the gazebo, chewing on the inside of my cheek.

"It was an obituary. She was writing her own obituary."

Maya's shoulders slumped. "How's Woof taking all of this?"

"Hard to say. Woof wouldn't talk about it—I'm sure of that. Come to think of it, I don't remember ever talking about those sorts of things with him. Not when his dad ran off. Never."

"But you're his best friend."

"Yeah. I kinda think that's why we don't talk about it. We don't need to. It's just there. He knows it. I know it. Talking doesn't fix anything. Somehow just being there is enough."

As we talked a sense of foreboding came over me. And that's when I noticed Spook almost hidden by the bushes. When I saw him he looked back at me with a stare so riveting I do not like to think of it even now. But there was more to it than that—something supernatural. Something was wrong, but I could not grasp what it was.

Later that night in bed, as I studied the ceiling cracks in the moon glow it came to me. I realized what it was that was so unusual about that moment in the park.

The birds had stopped singing.

We had all learned to live with the disconcerting moments Spook caused, and we joked about him sometimes because it made us feel better and braver than we were. But as the years passed, his madness progressed. You could feel it. And when he passed with his Thorazine gait that summer it was like a cloud passing the face of the sun. He radiated menace and the threat that with all the things he had done there was worse to come.

When he could, Tiny would railroad him off to the state hospital on trumped up charges. It wasn't legal, but no one argued that it wasn't the right thing to do. But Spook always returned, having been officially certified as uncommonly sane for a crazy son of a bitch, usually about the time the state hospital shrink started driving a new Caddy or his wife started sporting a mink coat in the grocery store, remarkable fiscal accomplishments, indeed, on a state shrink's salary.

Ernest Collins Jr. was Spook's real name. It sounds so innocuous when you say it, and I think in the beginning, folks around here tried to write him off as innocuous. Just a strange little boy. He graduated from box elder bug amputations to frog executions, but after his left-handed mother parked a .38 caliber hollow-point bullet in her brain with her *right hand*—ambidextrous for the first time as witnessed by her husband—that is when his soul went completely dark. Neighborhood pets started to vanish.

Then he developed a fixation with redheaded girls. His mother had been a striking auburn beauty in her time—a kind and decent woman, my mother said. "I don't think Spook would have become what he became if she had lived," she said.

The year she died was Tiny's first year as city cop. Murder charges were filed against Spook's old man, but the county prosecutor, Josh Rustan, bungled the job. Rustan was routinely out-lawyered by indignant little old ladies battling stop sign violations, so he was no match for the high-powered sharks Spook's old man could afford.

For a while, Tiny took the trouble to bring cases to court. Then, after the guilty walked free, Tiny would grouse, "We the people just got our ass whupped again."

But after Spook's old man was acquitted, Tiny began administering his own standard of justice. When he saw Spook stalking seventh grade girls on the way back from school, Tiny would find a way to bust him for something in order to get him back to the state hospital.

And every time old man Collins would find a way to get him released, not because he gave a rip about his son, but because he knew what a thorn in the side he was for Tiny. It was Spook ping-pong, and the hellhole position of state psychiatrist became a lucrative career, greased by the old man's formidable stack of cash accumulated over the years by the tragic yet well-insured losses of both parents and a daughter who succumbed to crib death at nine. I always figured the only reason Spook hadn't tumbled down the cellar stairs with scissors in his hand was that he was so damn much fun to have around.

After the fearsome beating he put on Coop, we expected that Spook would be locked up for good, but Spook's lawyer so confused Coop when he testified, it swayed one juror, a good Christian lady from a farm up north. She later explained to Gunnar Smithers and the *Pale Butte Sentinel* that "you can't trust a retard."

Then, as if to pour salt in the wound, Josh Rustan brought assault charges against Woof for the beating in the alley despite the fact that Tiny hadn't seen a thing. Rustan botched that case, too, so there's something to be said for consistency, I guess.

I never felt good about our style of vigilante justice, but it was the only justice we had. You couldn't blame Marty Leesburg for coming unglued the day twelve-year-old Ginger Leesburg wandered home with her clothes shredded, unable to speak about what had happened in the alley behind Spook's house.

Every night she would sit up and scream silent screams. Her mouth would open, but nothing would come out. Then she would shudder. Just shudder. Her red hair turned white before she was thirteen. But by that time she was permanently shelved in the state hospital—the same state hospital to which Spook was regularly exiled.

"It's nice Junior gets to visit her once in a while,"

Spook's old man whispered to Sarah Leesburg in Prunty's Store one day.

It took twenty-seven stitches to close the gash on his forehead made by a fourteen-ounce can of stewed tomatoes. There was lots of blood—bad blood.

And it was just as well that Marty Leesburg's Ranchero wasn't running so good when he saw what had happened to his little girl that day. He found Bertram Sumpter, who was liquored up—because it was after 3 P.M.—and they decided to drag Spook's ass to jail. Literally. One end of the rope was looped around Spook's legs, the other around the rear bumper, and they made it about a quarter mile out of town—because they were taking the long way—before the Ranchero sputtered to a stop. *Fuckin' fuel pump.*

There was a lot of skin on the ice-spackled road but not as much as there might have been had Spook not been wearing a parka and two pair of pants over long underwear. The dragging left a bloody spot the size of a silver dollar on the back of Spook's head where the hair and scalp had been worn away. The hair never grew back and the hole healed to a purplish-colored scar.

AND THEY DANCED

After supper on Friday, even though it was time for me to join the gang, I did what I had not done in a long time. I sat for a time with my family as I had so many evenings before, watching television.

That night it was *The Rockford Files*. From the davenport where he always reclined, Dad peered at the screen over his belly. The giant bowl of popcorn rested at his side on the floor. Coop sat on the brown braided rug beside the bowl, watching the black-and-white images broadcast pointlessly to us in living color. My parents did not upgrade to a color television until the old Zenith's flickering finally ceased sometime in the mid-eighties. Because black-and-white "was good enough," Dad said.

Mom sat like always in the padded rocker, knitting. The project had started out as mittens for a grade school nephew who by then was in his second year of college. The mittens grew into a scarf and then a sweater and then a blanket, and then she gave up trying to identify the thing at all.

Color had long since ceased to be an issue. She purchased skeins of yarn at the estate auctions of the little old ladies who had faded away, sometimes getting boxes of the stuff in the most awful hues for pennies. No matter how little she paid, Dad would survey the awful colors and grouse that she had been cheated.

Charlie Brown would eye my mother as she settled in with needles and yarn. And always she would admonish him. "Charlie, now don't you mess with this tonight!" Charlie's head would fall, his shoulders would slump, and he would look appropriately contrite. But when Mom was distracted by the television, Charlie would nonchalantly stretch and slither like an infantryman behind her chair and begin unraveling the other end. When he was a pup, the unraveling had been playful. Now, it was as if it was his job, and he approached it like a world-weary comic after years on the road delivering stale material, two shows a night.

Coop, Dad, and I shared knowing glances as we watched Charlie, but we never ratted him out. Mom pretended obliviousness, but when the final credits rolled and she rose to hide the shameful thing, she would spot the loops Charlie had pulled loose and she would admonish him, speaking to him in the most formal of tones as she did to us when we had erred.

"Charles W. Brown!" Nobody knew what the W stood for. "How would you like to sleep outside tonight?" Charlie would cock his head, pretending not to understand and fully confident the threat would never become reality. He would wag his stump of a tail. Mom would sigh and try not to smile. Some nights Charlie pulled loose more than she had knitted, but in Charlie's later years, her stamina exceeded his, so mostly she gained a few stitches, and the thing grew.

The Oglala Sioux have a legend of a woman who weaves a porcupine quillwork in the moonlight as a kettle of herbs boils beside her. When she rises to tend to the kettle, stirring it, her dog unravels the work. It is said that if she ever completes the quillwork, the world will end at that instant.

It was 9:30 when we heard the rumble of the Chevy for the third time as Woof trolled past the house. This time he dropped it into first gear abruptly and the car backfired, popping and banging. I rose to walk to the front porch steps to wait for Woof's next orbit.

"Where do you think you're going?" my father barked, the way he had when I lived under his roof and he actually had a say in the matter. But now, it had become a tradition—a brusque, circuitous way of saying that he cared, and though he never said it, that he loved me.

"Well, I'm going to drink some beer, chase girls, and me and Woof were thinking maybe later on if things get slow, we'll rob the bank."

Dad grunted his approval, still stretched out on his davenport throne. Thus, I was excused. Coop followed me out and we sat as the comfortable, warm cloak of evening enveloped Pale Butte.

"I have to cut Sela Rosemount's lawn tomorrow," Coop said.

"You'll probably be able to retire after that."

Coop grinned. Sela Rosemount lived alone in the only home in town built of fieldstones. It was a magnificent home and a perfect fit for Sela, who was as cold and tough as the stones—at least that was the act. There were rumors of kindnesses, most unsubstantiated. But over the years, she had taken less fortunate children under her wing, most recently Tanya Schwartz, giving her piano lessons, and in exchange, Tanya retrieved and then returned three books a week to the Emma Bernham Memorial Library from Emma herself, who at ninety-two, had run the library so long, Mayor Bull Malone decided to name it in her honor. "You could have waited until I was dead," she complained, certain that the memorial part of the new name meant she was a goner for sure. But she made it to a hundred and five before drifting away at her desk at the library, a hot and naughty romance bookmarked beside her.

But even when Tanya Schwartz's belly swelled and the rest of the old ladies gossiped and shunned her, tough old Sela Rosemount stuck by the girl, even to the point of joining her on an errand or two uptown in a display of solidarity. Tanya offered an arm of support as Sela grouched along on her swollen gout-ravaged legs during these rare public appearances, ordering clerks around, complaining about the inferior quality of the goods, and in general upholding her reputation as a Class A battle-ax.

"Coop, now you make sure you trim every blade of grass around every tree. You know how Sela is. She'll pay you well, but she expects perfection."

"Okay."

I could hear Woof's Chevy approaching. As he down-shifted, the mufflers rat-a-tated like machine-gun fire. I stood and walked to the street to wait for the car. Maya was sitting in the middle between Woof and Butch, which relegated me to the backseat. Butch made an exaggerated show of throwing his arm around my girl.

She snuggled close just to rub it in.

"I guess the wedding is off, huh?" I said.

"Not at all, darrrling," Maya said, rolling her Rs like Zsa Zsa Gabor. "I'm just comforting the garrrdenerrr. It seems he has discovered weeds in the rutabagas. He's completely in-consolable."

Butch put on a hangdog look for effect. And then he winked.

She left me alone back there for a good while, too.

Later that night we found ourselves at Joe Big Cloud's. Peggy Lee was sashaying through the speakers when Joe opened the door to let us in. We all sat in the usual places, Woof and I at the chessboard, Butch and Maya with Joe on the couch. But first Joe had to evict the dirty white lamb from the cushions where it had been curled up like a house cat. The lamb stretched, pranced a few feet, and lay back down on the mat by the door.

"That the gimpy one?" I asked. Joe nodded.

I guess I had known the answer. I snagged a bishop and was four pieces up on Woof, which made me nervous as I sorted through the maze of possibilities. You could never be sure exactly when Woof's concentration had slipped or when it was an elaborate trap. So even in a game in which you were waxing his ass, you could never really enjoy it until he tipped his king in defeat. He was the source of more paranoia than anyone I have ever known.

"Joe," Maya wondered, as she sat on the floor stroking the lamb, "did you ever try to heal people?" Instantly, she knew it was a bad question because a kind of flintiness came to Joe's usually imperturbable face. Woof slowly turned in his chair to look at Joe and then at Maya and the lamb. There was not one of us in the room who did not know what he was thinking. What he was hoping.

"Is that all there is?" Peggy Lee intruded from the speakers, and then she repeated the question, singing it this time. Joe stared out the window. I shifted in my seat. Butch stared at the speaker, pretending the moment was not becoming unbearably uncomfortable. But Maya continued to look at Joe expectantly. I suppose it was less than a minute, but it felt like centuries before Joe deflated a little, looked at Maya, and then right into Woof's eyes. "Once," he said.

We waited and I doubt any of us was breathing.

"She was old, and it was hard for me to see her suffer. I was just learning to use the gift in those days. A great medicine man was teaching me because he thought I was blessed. I wanted to help. I was desperate to do so because I loved the old woman. But she became angry with me. 'Do not block my journey,' she said. 'This is the path I must travel.'

"I tried to understand," Joe said. "But all I could imagine was my sorrow when she was gone. I was selfish, and I tried to change her mind.

"This is what she said to me: 'Silly medicine man, do not intrude in this sacred place. Do not delay my chance for atonement. Things are as they should be. What shall I gain from this? Let me go.'

"When she was too weak to argue with me anymore, though, I tried to draw the sickness out of her. But it made me weak like no healing had ever done before. It was like death, itself. I was scared, so I stopped."

He paused, and then continued slowly as if the weight of each word might crush him if he spoke too many. "I was ashamed of my fear. Of my weakness. Of my shallow faith. Still, I went to my teacher to tell him what I had done and to see if he would save her.

"This is what he told me: 'Healing in this world is a temporary thing. The old woman seeks healing of her spirit. She is walking this path to be closer to the Great Mystery. You cannot force a gift upon her if she chooses not to accept it.'

"I have tried to remember that," Joe said. "And I understand now that the healing must start from within."

"Then what is it that you do?" Maya asked.

"I call the spirits. I am the connection."

"And the old woman died?"

Joe nodded, and his lips opened as if he was contemplating whether he should tell us more. He looked at each of us and then he looked away. When he spoke, the voice seemed to come from somewhere else.

"She was my mother."

Woof's eyes fell and he sucked in an involuntary breath that sounded like the yelp of a puppy. We pretended not to notice.

"Do you think you could have saved her if she had wanted it?" Maya asked.

Joe wrung his hands, staring at them. "I don't know. I don't know if my faith is that strong. That's the truth of it."

He rose sadly and walked to the turntable, and I realized only then that the music had stopped. The needle floated down to fresh vinyl, and Ol' Blue Eyes began to croon.

Maya rose and glided over to Joe. "May I have this dance?"

Astaire took her hand and placed his other on her hip. They began to sway to the music. Some days I look back and I see them in my mind, Maya and Joe, dancing in perfect step. I hear her laugh like a giddy child as he twirls her, her mouth wide, teeth shining white, eyes closed in some sublime ecstasy. I see Joe—*who knew Joe could dance*—I see the baggy work pants masking the graceful actions of his legs.

And I see Joe smile.

Sometimes as I stroll across the prairie, looking at the giant wind machines grinding out energy in the distance, I see Joe and Maya floating across the tall grass below the blades chopping at the air and I hear the music on the wind. It is hard to convince myself that they are not really there.

There are rare moments in this world when the usual halting stutter of life is transcended for a moment by poetry and symmetry, and everything feels perfect. I look back, and my heart glows and still aches a bit for Maya and the poetry that swirled around her—the poetry she created.

And I smile.

When the song ended and Joe's hand fell from her hip, Maya leaned and kissed Joe on the cheek. Then she walked to me and offered her hand. I took it and stood, and she led me to the door.

The girl knew how to make an exit.

The lamb stood, too, as if it were coming along. Then the tail rose and hot, round turds were deposited on Joe's floor. So much for the poetry of the moment.

"There you go, Joe," Butch said in that laconic drawl. "Payment in full for services rendered." The ingrate was back in the pasture the next day.

A DREAM SO REAL

She was kissing me. Passionate kisses. And the dream was so real I could feel it. The surprising thing was it was Martha J. Wilcox. I almost woke up from the guilt of cheating on Maya, but it was such a good dream, so delicious, I dove right back in. Arms around me, breasts squished against my chest, one leg between mine, she was slowly humping my knee. When she licked my ear in a long delicious slurp, it felt so real I had to open my eyes.

I awoke to find Charlie Brown staring down at me, I swear, with the biggest damn doggie grin, and a long, dangling string of dog drool that landed right on my lips. Coop cackled as I wiped my face on the sheets, spitting and gagging as I squinted at the mute alarm clock.

"Geez, Coop, it's not even six o'clock."

"You said we were going fishing this morning!"

"At nine, Coop. At nine! There is a difference, you know."

In Coop's world, sixes and nines were interchangeable. The truth was, fishing was usually more productive at six than at nine, but my morning evolution to something resembling a human was rarely complete until nine. I started to get out of bed but stopped, realizing a tent had formed in my underwear, and I sure wasn't up to explaining *that* to Coop at 5:48 A.M. Fine. The stupid dog had given me a woody. As Coop wandered about my apartment, I pulled my pants on over the subsiding erection, still thinking about Martha and the dream, and then, rudely, about Charlie Brown licking my ear. I started to feel a little queasy.

If we had gone fishing at nine, we would have missed Joe, so once I got moving, I couldn't complain about the way things worked out. The mist was so heavy that morning you could almost drink it.

Joe patiently tied fresh hooks to Coop's line after each snag. Eyeing Coop warily, the old snapper waited on the dam for the sun to crest the trees along the river. Coop absently fingered his scar.

"I hate that turtle!" Coop blurted.

Joe nodded. "Did you know that if it wasn't for the turtle, there would be no land for you to fish upon?" he asked.

"Really?"

"Yes. My mother told me about it when I was a small boy. You see, long ago there was a world before this one. It was a beautiful place. But people did not behave themselves."

"Like Spook," Coop said.

"Like Spook," Joe agreed. "Grandfather grew sad that his people were behaving so badly. That they were abusing the beautiful earth he had created for them. In time, his sadness turned to anger, and he resolved to wash away the evil of the world."

"Sometimes I think the world is a very bad place," Coop said. "I see it on TV."

"Yes," said Joe. "There are many with dark hearts today just as there were then, so Grandfather began to sing songs to bring rain. With each rain song it rained harder. And harder still. With the fourth rain song, the earth split open and water flowed up and flooded the land. All of the people were drowned, and most of the animals, too. One crow was flying. He watched from above. Then he realized there was no place for him to land. He would be doomed to circle the earth, flapping his wings forever. So he pleaded with Grandfather to give him a place to rest."

Joe flapped his arms for effect and cackled from the back of his throat like a crow, "I am so tired!" Coop grinned.

"Grandfather had pity on the crow," Joe continued. "He decided that he would create a new world. A better world. So he reached into his pipe bag and pulled out creatures well known for their ability to remain under water for a very long time. First, he sent the loon under water to retrieve mud to build the land upon. But the water was too deep for the loon, and he failed. The otter tried very hard, too. But he could not hold his breath long enough. The beaver, with his strong flat tail, got close, but he, too, failed. He came splashing to the surface, gasping for breath. At last Grandfather pulled the turtle from his pipe bag. The turtle stayed under water for a very long time. So long that the others grew sad because they were sure he had perished. Then, after a very long time there was a big splash."

"The turtle!" Coop cheered.

"The turtle. And the turtle's claws were full of mud. Grandfather took the mud and molded it into a small island so the weary crow could rest. Then Grandfather waved magic eagle feathers over the land, and it grew much larger. But when he was finished, Grandfather looked out over the land and saw that it was dry and barren. Lifeless. A great sadness overwhelmed him, and he began to weep. His tears formed puddles, which formed lakes and rivers, and the land came alive with growth. It could not have happened without the humble turtle.

" 'For what you have done,' Grandfather told the turtle, 'you will be forever remembered. This continent shall be known as the Turtle Continent. And until the arrival of the next world, this continent will be shaped like a turtle.'

"So you see," Joe continued, "the turtle is actually a pretty good fellow."

"Yeah, but he bites hard," Coop said.

Joe caught a stringer full of bullheads and two needle-toothed northern pike. Coop caught four trees, a log, seven fat bullheads, and Joe's pant leg, and I caught a few extra winks on a bed of cattails. Just a few. It was hard to sleep with Coop's hooks whistling overhead.

I finally gave up when he began singing, "Shall we gather at the river . . ." in his tone-deaf monotone. Still, considering we were actually at the river and all, it was kind of fitting. "Where did you learn the song?" I asked.

"Momma's been practicing," Coop said. "Reverend Lomas asked her to sing in church." He hummed a few lines tunelessly until he remembered more of the words. "I wonder why Reverend Lomas doesn't ask *me* to sing," he said. He looked at me and then at Joe, who got a panicked look.

"It's a mystery," Joe said.

A BREACH OF LOYALTY

Reverend Lomas K. Brown was the first spark of energy the congregation had seen from the pulpit in years. Anyone would have been an improvement over Reverend Jorgensen, whose intellect and vocabulary were so superior to his flock it became the only church in the state where you could see as many people toting dictionaries as Bibles into the pews.

"Be thee an adherent not to the abominations and hedonism of terra firma but harken instead to the melodious strains of scriptures divine and epistles most holy delivered here by the revered discarnates."

"What the hell did he say?"

"Don't sin and read the Bible."

When Lomas was called to serve fresh out of seminary, swarthy and handsome, with a crown of ebony hair and cool blue eyes under prominent black eyebrows swooping across his forehead, speaking actual English, he was embraced. Whispering old ladies swooned and blushed, because he looked a little dangerous like a young Brando. Even Ella Peterson, who had sworn off the Lord after losing three husbands to various ailments in an eleven-year span, returned to church.

I liked him, too, and so did Woof. It was not uncommon for Lomas to invite us over for a bachelor-cooked mess of deer sausage and fried potatoes. We would thank the Lord for his bounty, and then Lomas would crack a beer. When he took us fishing on Dry Lake in his creaky old Alumacraft, he always brought a cooler of Grain Belt.

That was the down-to-earth side of Lomas we liked. But it always seemed to me that Lomas hadn't been entirely ready for the pious path of preacherhood. I think sometimes he struggled to believe lock, stock, and barrel everything he was supposed to stand for. So he would bounce from good old boy to near zealotry from the guilt of being human and horny. And when she moved next door, Lomas took a real interest in comforting the widow Martha Wilcox at unusual hours.

That was the rumor.

The church ladies gossiped, and the deacons mumbled about Reverend Brown's variances from the approved Lutheran path, but in the beginning, the insurgency was small. The pews on Sunday were so full, if you were late, you got a tan folding chair or you ended up in the organ loft. The offerings were bountiful.

If Lomas tripped over his hormones now and then, his great weakness was his anger. It was there always, bubbling beneath his tan and in the flash of his blue eyes. He would explode in rage in an instant. He was entirely forthcoming about it. Once he had launched a javelin at a teammate who had taunted him in a Nebraska track meet. It was a story he told often, entertained by the near miss, grateful and horrified all the same.

"If I had thrown it that far in actual competition, I would have won that day. It sailed past his shoulder," he said. "I suppose I would still be in jail."

Woof was a victim of that rage not long after Lomas came to town. One day at the lake Lomas and a dozen Luther Leaguers were at the dock waiting our turn to ski behind Lomas' sluggish thirty-five-horse Johnson outboard. Lomas was waist deep, concentrating on the tangle of the towrope, when Woof playfully dunked him. No big deal.

But Lomas exploded like a hydra from the water and in one swift motion, grabbed Woof by the shoulders and pushed him hard below the surface and held him there until Woof's thrashing began to ebb, and I was convinced I was witnessing a murder. The rest of us stood there shocked at the deranged look on Lomas' face.

Finally, Lomas pulled him up and Woof emerged, sputtering and gasping desperately for breath. He was wide-eyed. It was a rare humiliating moment for my friend.

The way Woof floated through life and the consistency of his miraculous victories had led most of us to believe he was blessed. Untouchable. Everything always seemed to go his way.

But 1977 was a cruel year. It was hard enough when his sister Tanya's belly started to round and swell until the new life growing within was obvious, but the heartbreak and embarrassment it caused the dying Rose Schwartz was the worst of it.

Tanya would not reveal the father's name.

These things happened from time to time, over the years in Pale Butte, like they have since the invention of babies. There were whirlwind marriages, dutifully noted on the calendars of the busybodies who would gossip viciously seven months later when healthy full-term babies arrived.

Sometimes young girls took "vacations." Some of these vacations were short, and they would return with empty eyes, and for a long time, if ever, they would not be the same.

A vacation was out of the question for Tanya Schwartz. As Rose was weakened by her cancer, the girl carried more of the load, and when the soft moans floated down the hallway at night, Tanya soothed her mother, brushing away dry wisps of graying hair.

It had been just the three of them since old man Schwartz stepped out for a pack of cigarettes and never came back when Woof was thirteen. That's when the pool table hustles began. Times were tough, but Woof had his pride. They could have gotten on the county dole, but Woof would have no part of it.

Still, folks will find a way to help. Mrs. Bull Malone, the regal Emily, decreed soon after Louis Schwartz, his pack of Kools, and a local trollop wandered off that she was in dire need of a housekeeper. Rose Schwartz was the first and last interview.

The pay was modest because small-town bankers cannot appear too ostentatious. It doesn't look good. Still, Tanya confided to me, her mother could never seem to reconcile her checking account at the Third National Bank. It would not balance. It was always long, and when she called to straighten it out, the teller always advised her the mistake was hers—certainly not the bank's—and that was that.

"Don't you dare tell Woof," Tanya ordered. I nodded, knowing full well that out of pride he would have demanded the account be moved to a bank where there were no such inconsistencies. Even when the cancer had forced Rose to take leave until she recovered, as Emily ordered sternly, the mysterious overages in the Schwartz account continued.

Tanya was the third pregnant teen of the summer, a high-water mark for Pale Butte. They were all Lutherans and the Reverend Lomas K. Brown took it personally. He lashed out in righteous indignation. One Sunday, Lomas delivered an old-fashioned fire-and-brimstone sermon about the evils of premarital sex, the wages of sin and whoring, and everyone knew who he was talking about, including Tanya and Rose Schwartz, sitting in their usual pew.

"Tanya left in tears in the middle of the sermon," my mother told us over Sunday dinner that day. My father, in his usual elevator standards, his hair askew from sleeping in, shifted in his creaky oak chair at the head of the table.

"What did Rose do?"

"She just took it. But when she passed Reverend Brown on the way out, she wouldn't shake his hand."

My father chewed the inside of his cheek. Coop drew a cross in the gravy remains on his plate.

"Lomas ain't quite right upstairs," my father said, tapping his temple.

What Lomas had done without ever understanding was an act of war.

With Woof, the issue was loyalty. Even after the Luther League drubbing, Woof had spent more time with Lomas than you expect an outlaw would, but I don't think Lomas ever understood the rules. They were fishing buddies and out here, that means something. Out here on the plains, a friend is a friend, and even when they're wrong—dead wrong—you stick by them and their kin. It is our code. Loyalty does not have to make sense.

The sermon humiliated Tanya and crushed Rose's spirit, a betrayal of the highest order, and I could not begin to imagine what Woof had in store for Lomas K. Brown. He did not say a word about it to me, but I could see the wheels turning. So you can imagine how surprised I was when two weeks after the sermon, as if nothing had ever happened, Woof Schwartz went fishing with the Reverend Lomas K. Brown.

A BETTER QUALITY
OF BAD THINGS

Love is not supposed to be complicated. That is the illusion. But the fact is, it is not a singular thing you can direct at the perfect girl or the ultimate god. The thing is, the mind wanders, it doubts and it questions.

That summer Maya floated in without an inkling of my place in the pecking order and declared me a prince. Like a massive ship slowing, turning, barely avoiding the icebergs, then steaming confidently toward a tropical climate, the course of my life was changed by a smart-aleck, long-legged redhead with wise, soft eyes.

Don't think that everyone in Pale Butte didn't notice, too, that suddenly I was the lucky one. Sure, she was only seventeen, but even the most cynical soul could see that she was something extraordinary.

I was too caught up wondering what would go wrong to notice the subtle changes around me and within me. But as I sift through it now, it seems that people began to treat me just a little bit better—and it's not that folks ever really treated me badly; it's just that somehow Maya had waved that wand and given me a certain credibility.

Funny how someone can come into your life and believe in you the way Maya did, and pretty soon you start to believe in yourself—*because you have to respect their opinion.* Then, as your confidence grows, people sense it, smell it, or whatever, and in the most imperceptible ways, more good things than bad start happening. If nothing else, a better quality of bad things start happening, and you find yourself dropping Cadillacs off the hoist instead of Edsels.

But you don't see it until later. Farmers don't know that the drought has ended just because you get a little drizzle one night. You need a series of sprinkles and a gully washer or two with lightning that dazzles the sky and splinters telephone poles.

And thunder. You need thunder to rattle the windows, to announce that if you survive the storm, things are gonna change.

But let's get back to my point about love. It's supposed to be this perfect thing and it isn't. It just isn't. You would think that having the perfect girl stroll into your life would complete you. You imagine that if it happens—and Lord knows, it rarely does—you will grab her hand, hold on tight, slap a ring on that finger, and know there is a God.

So why was I dreaming about Martha? I mean, *you* know why I was dreaming about Martha. That throaty voice, the deep brown eyes peeking past blond bangs she grew a little too long, like she was hiding back there. You'd have to be dead not to dream about that package. But under the circumstances, having the most spectacular creature I had ever seen love me, and then cheating on her—even if it was in a dream—well, it made me feel like a complete heel.

If it had just been the dream, one stray dream, I could have soothed my conscience. I could have written it off as a misfiring neuron in my brain someplace, a symptom of bad hops in the malt liquor. But the truth is, I thought about Martha a lot. And after Maya inexplicably chose me, I thought of Martha even more. Human beings can be such dirtbags. At least I'd like to think I'm not the only one. On the other hand, the world would be a better place if I were. Why is it that the more you have, the more you want? Now, I appreciate the wisdom of detachment. Of course, it's easier now that my hormones have run their course.

I haven't figured it out, but my best guess is that when you find yourself at a crossroad, you stall, no matter how inviting one direction might look, because you don't want to make the wrong decision. Sometimes the inviting road isn't the one you are supposed to travel. For whatever reason it just doesn't *feel* right. Sometimes you choose the bumpier, less obvious road.

Loving Maya was like trying to hold the wind.

I had imagined more than once, as Maya and I wrestled, hands stroking, tension rising, panting—I imagined her tummy growing, her face glowing, and a baby boy cementing us into a family. It was a destiny I would have reveled in.

We would have been together forever.

As I imagined that future though, in my mind I could see her looking wistfully outside, ignoring the chatter of our son. The walls and the windows in my vision melted and were replaced by the brass bars of a birdcage. Somewhere inside I knew that even if our love was right, the timing was not. I knew she could not become what she was destined to be if I held her back.

So I did not take advantage of her. I could not. And I wonder often if I did the right thing. I wonder if I should have let her go.

With Martha it was different. I did not doubt that granted the invitation, I would leap to her embrace, that I would burrow into her soft breasts. Yet, despite her flirtations, I could never be sure that it was not just a game she played to remind herself of her desirability. The town was littered with the carcasses of the rejected, and I didn't want to be one of them. So, it seemed best to not risk a foolish gambit and close the door completely. I wasn't sure I could take that. Better to keep hope alive. Better to let the possibilities roam in my dreams.

Like I said, love isn't simple. It isn't tidy. Sometimes a relationship thrives on passion and romance. Sometimes it's plain old loyalty that keeps you together until something reignites the flame or extinguishes it completely.

Love is fluid.

You can't box it.

You can't hold it.

You can't control it.

It pisses me off.

Sometimes love becomes more about status than anything. I saw a hint of that in the way my relationship with Maya raised my standing in Pale Butte. People see you with someone special, and they start to figure that *you* must be special. And if you find that gal or guy, as the case may be, and you *each* think the other is the special one, that is when love is as close to perfect as it's ever going to be.

Mostly, as I look around and from my perch, I see that a lot of lovebirds aren't really in love. Marriage becomes more of a business arrangement.

I know I say time and time again that I am an optimist, yet here I sit all cynical about romance. At the very least, I have to allow that I am a cynical optimist. Or maybe, more of a realist than an optimist. But realistically (and cynically) speaking, I see four reasons for marriage. You throw your hands up in the air after a while and you decide, "Hey, I have to have *somebody*!" So you get impatient waiting for the right one, and you compromise so you don't have to be alone. Or there is true love, the rarest kind, and sometimes even that doesn't work out. Sometimes you have to let them go. And sometimes it's the right thing.

Then there's marriage for money. Security. When you see a twenty-six-year-old knockout marry an eighty-year-old man, you can be damn sure it isn't because she has a thing for liver spots. That sort of thing isn't natural. And there's status. Folks marry for status—status and money.

Diana Sturm Roberts got both. She left Pale Butte the

day after she graduated as Diana Sturm, and I hadn't seen her since. I hadn't missed her, either.

I was picking up a package of minced ham at Prunty's Store when I saw her at the other end of the meat counter. I didn't see her face right away, and her hair was different, a little shorter and slightly curled, but I knew it was her just by the way she carried herself. She was Pale Butte royalty, self-appointed, and I can't pretend that I didn't carry some resentment toward her which began back early in high school when "The Doc of Rock" was spinning records for a homecoming dance at the Pale Butte Auditorium.

She was sitting with her particular clique of prissy girlfriends—Diana and the Supremes, Woof called them—when I walked up and asked her to dance. After all, she *was* pretty with straight, long black hair and porcelain skin.

She said no. She was too tired from *all* the dancing she had done.

I guess every girl has a right to say no. But it didn't happen much. Even the princesses in the Dakotas generally respect the manners their mommas taught them, and they dance, albeit reluctantly, with the frogs. But after I walked away to the giggles of the Supremes, Whitey walked up, and she danced with *him*.

In that moment, Diana had branded me a second-class citizen, and the Supremes followed suit, and it became clear to me in ways you can feel more than substantiate that that particular class of girl was off-limits to me.

"Bones!" she called that day in the store, like nothing

had ever happened, like we were long lost friends. "I thought that was you!"

I managed a weak smile.

"So what *are* you doing nowadays?"

"You know, same old thing. Working at Farmers Union. Listening to Marv cuss. Pounding out a few stories for the newspaper."

I paused as she stood there, her eyes wide open as if she was really enthralled with the new and exciting turns my life had taken. I paused because I knew what I was supposed to ask, and I just didn't want to hear the answer. But she continued to look up at me, perfect and plastic, like I was the most interesting person she had seen all day, and she broke my will. I could not stand the silence. So I asked.

"What brings you back, Diana?"

Like a torrent it came. All the wonderful and impressive things she had done and seen while I had been imbedding grease so deep into my calluses they would not come clean.

"And you know I'm married now?"

"Really?" (Poor bastard.)

"Yes, for two years." She waved a big honkin' diamond in my face.

"He's a dentist."

"Of course he is." The smile faded for a second, but she recovered and resumed her perky stare-down, waiting for me to stumble and stammer and turn red like I usually did under intense cross-examination.

I noticed Gerber rice cereal in her hand. "I guess you married him young."

The smile faded again, and again she recovered with a forced shriek of laughter that deposited a bit of spittle on my chin. I pretended not to notice. "Bones, you haven't changed. You are still so funny!"

(Yeah, I am.)

"Of course, you knew Stanley and I had a baby, didn't you?"

Of course, I knew. The whole damn town knew. There had been a picture of the kid two columns wide on the front page of the *Pale Butte Sentinel* about six months ago. I guess it was pretty big news. Diana Sturm Roberts had given birth, and the progeny was actually human.

"His name is Maurice . . ."

(Uh, huh.)

"And he is sooo handsome."

I smiled. The little shit didn't stand a chance. Maurice! They named him Maurice? Why didn't they just name him Kick My Ass and get it over with?

"Anyway, Maurice is being baptized on Sunday. We wanted to bring him back to my hometown for that. It would just be so much more meaningful."

I nodded, my eyes just as wide as hers, pursing my lips just to show her I was every bit as excited about this whole thing as she was.

"We should have been back months ago. But Stanley's

practice has just been exploding! We just haven't been able to get away. He has even been working Saturdays to keep up."

I was having a hard time holding my smile. Sure, Stanley was working a lot. Who wouldn't want to spend all day sucking in the fumes of rotting teeth and periodontal disease when the alternative was listening to this mindless blather? I began slowly making my way toward the checkout where Sally Prunty was chomping gum in a soiled green smock and leaning over a copy of *True Story*. Diana walked with me, and when we got there, I waved her ahead.

Sally punched in the numbers on the giant gold cash register, which was probably as old as she was. "Seventy-three cents."

Diana pulled an American Express Travelers Cheque out of her clutch purse and signed it over. Sally picked it up and frowned. "I don't think I have change for a hundred. I'll have to step next door to the bank."

"Look, let me get it," I said, digging into my pocket, not willing to extend the ordeal of this interminable conversation. Geez, it was worth seventy-three cents, easy.

"Absolutely not. I wouldn't think of it," Diana said, so Sally shrugged and left the store to us. So I learned that Diana and Stanley and the doomed Maurice had a wonderful new home in a wonderful new neighborhood in Littleton. It's a suburb of Denver, you know, and that traffic is just so unbelievable as you drive your BMW to the market where they have absolutely everything! And there is the theater (thea ah tuh), the symphony, the zoo, and the museum, and *why do you stick around here anyway, Bones?*

Several years later, Sally returned from the Third National Bank of Pale Butte, still smacking her gum. Even after she received her ninety-nine dollars and twenty-seven cents, Diana continued to yap. Didn't she need to breathe sometime?

"You should come to the baptism."

(Oh, Lordy, I should. I'm real big on baptisms.)

"I would love to introduce you to Stanley. He just loves it here."

"Yes, our dust is quite impressive."

"Ha! But really Stanley says everything here is so . . . *quaint*! And he and Reverend Brown just hit it off! Lomas invited him to go fishing at Dry Lake with him and Woof on Saturday. Stanley is so excited. He's never been fishing before."

"I'll bet he'll be real good at removing the hooks," I said.

I tried to eat the minced ham a couple times, but I could never bring myself to bring it close to my mouth even after I had taken the time to make the sandwich. It seemed tainted by Diana's presence.

Charlie Brown had no such qualms about it, though. He wolfed it down in three quick gulps, eyeing me like it might be some sort of trick and that I might pull it back. I guess even dogs understand that when things are going good, they can change in a heartbeat.

THE BAPTISM

If the Reverend Lomas K. Brown had considered Woof's apparent benevolence, he might have thought Woof had forgiven him. Or maybe Woof agreed with his stand against pregnant little Lutheran girls, and how it made it look like no one was really listening to the word of God you laid down each Sunday. And if there wasn't a specific commandment against teen pregnancy, there sure as hell should have been.

Go ahead.

Be fruitful and multiply.

After you're eighteen and married.

And then, don't enjoy it.

But I doubt Lomas gave it much thought at all. Maybe for a moment he wondered why a guy like Woof, vengeful as the Old Testament God Himself with a toothache and a bagful of pestilence, hadn't at least *said something*. But more than likely, Lomas was as obtuse as we all are as we parade through life like steers through the chutes on their way to slaughter.

It's easier to pretend that nothing's going to happen. When you're young and strong, and piss and vinegar courses through your veins, you can't fathom mortality.

The steers do not know the day they are led to slaughter. They stroll through the pasture, getting fat, chewing grains and vitamin supplements, too.

They learn to run the chutes early on in life. Sometimes veterinarians wait at the end with needles as thick as tenpenny nails. Horns get lopped off in fine mists of blood. A quick cut, and bullish dreams of meadow romances end. Steers are trucked or herded from one pasture to another after the first is chewed down and trampled. There are always more chutes and some kind of discomfort, some as minor as a ladle of cold chemical brew to keep the flies from pestering off the pounds.

Some animals fight and leap high to try to clear the steel bars and that gets men hurt. Pointy-toed boots are stomped, slow-moving hands are mashed, and rage erupts sometimes. Wooden canes and whips descend on the backs of animals. Prods shock and jolt them forward anyway.

Most of the animals hardly fuss at all. They go through the chutes, take whatever medicine is being forced upon them for the day, and a few minutes later all is forgotten and they're grazing in the cool deep grass. It's just another day.

It was a grand day on Dry Lake. Stanley Roberts, DDS, landed a five-pound walleye, a couple three-pounders, and a slimy twenty-nine-pound northern pike which appeared a week later on the front page of the *Pale Butte Sentinel,* a full column width wider than the birth of Stanley and Diana's first child.

Lomas and Woof pulled in their usual limit, and the Alumacraft dragged two heavy stringers back to the dock that evening. It took Lomas a good fifteen minutes to back the trailer up because Woof had suggested a celebratory toast of Redeye after each fish—Redeye is 190-proof Everclear with a little burnt sugar and a dash of grenadine mixed in to take the edge off. After seven fish, they started toasting successful casts.

Lomas drove the thirteen miles back swerving from one lane to the other. But, being a preacher and all, he was not likely to get arrested.

On a typical day, with a sharp blade, Woof and Lomas could fillet two dozen fish in forty-five minutes and be slapping tartar sauce beside the meat in an hour. But with Woof encouraging toasts along the way, the process took nearly three hours, and if there was a blessing to be had in all of this, it was that no one lost a thumb.

It took the dentist four years and two dozen roses every Mother's Day and birthday, Easter, and Valentine's Day before his mother-in-law began to thaw. I have seen corpses less pale than Stanley Roberts was for his son's baptism. He might have missed the whole thing, but near as I can figure, the angels intervened and awakened him, sprawled out on the carpet of the parsonage, forty-five minutes before the scheduled service.

Diana had covered for her perfect husband, explaining he was out for his morning walk, and maybe Fred and Janice Sturm bought the story at first, because the man was, after all, *a dentist,* but when the screen door slammed and Stanley commandeered the only bathroom in the house for a full fifteen minutes doing what sounded like dinosaur calls, Fred, the church council president and a suspicious man, figured it out.

That morning, I was up early, too. The phone awakened me on the couch.

"Get up," Woof said when I reached the phone on the thirtieth ring, convinced that anyone that persistent at that hour was going to inform me of some sort of tragedy.

"Uhh, wah, uhh," I said with my usual morning eloquence.

"We're going to church."

Oh, that. Sure. Just another Sunday morning at church with Woof. I hadn't seen him all night, and apparently in his absence, Woof had been saved. Hallelujah. I didn't bother to argue. For one thing, I was unable, at that time of the morning, to form complete sentences. For another, I never won an argument with Woof, anyway.

Jesus, where were my wingtips? I sure as hell wasn't going in greasy lace-up work boots. Woof was pretty irritated by the time I found them. He was dapper in his brown suit and wide lime green tie, but if you looked close, you could see his complexion was the hue of his tie. Like he was going through photosynthesis or something.

The heat almost knocked me over when I stepped outside. If it was sweltering outside, inside the church it was stifling. Sunlight leaned oppressively through stained glass onto the bodies wedged tightly in the pews. In unison, almost every head turned when we walked in during the final stanza of the first hymn. They looked again, as we noisily set up two tan folding chairs behind the last full pew. Lomas, who usually sang loud and proud, appeared to be mouthing the words, badly out of sync like the dialogue in a bad Italian western. Rose Schwartz looked back, too, and smiled wanly, pleased that her son had seen the light.

Tanya was absent. Again.

Beside me, Woof grimaced as I turned the pages trying to follow along. I discovered too late that the reading was in the bulletin, which had an extraordinary number of typos. Either that or the church ladies really were going to be holding a benefit *hop dish susser for the Smptrs* (Sumpters), to help them rebuild after the fire.

And now, apparently, there had been the tragic loss of their vowels.

Lomas moved like a man walking through sand. In the front row, the Sturm family stared straight ahead and didn't turn even at the clatter of our chairs. Diana's hair was piled high and perfect. Stanley pulled off his jacket like a dozen other men, and I could see his white shirt was soaked clear through.

I couldn't put my finger on it, but Lomas looked a little weird. I mean, I had started to connect the dots between

Woof and Stanley and Lomas. Even Dr. Watson could have figured this one out, and the fact that Woof had dragged me to church at all meant *something* was going on. I just couldn't figure out what it was.

But Lomas looked different. It wasn't just the hangover.

When he moved closer to the baptismal font, I could see what it was. There was a black smudge over his left eye, and as he spoke, commanding the sponsors about their holy duties to the protesting young Maurice Roberts, the smudge began to spread with the sweat from his brow.

Woof sat forward, elbowed me, and grinned. Then I could see. Lomas Brown was missing an eyebrow, and what looked like mascara was beginning to run.

"What happened to him?" I whispered.

"I might have accidentally shaved his eyebrow off while he was passed out," Woof said. Then he sputtered, trying to hold back the laughter. A few testy old ladies whiplashed their heads around to deliver disapproving glares at us.

"So why did you shave off just one?" I asked.

"Artistic license."

As the mascara smeared, Lomas began to resemble Alice Cooper looming over a Billion Dollar Baby even as he spoke of eternal life and the grace of God. Diana held the child over the font because Stanley, visibly shaky, might have dropped the lad.

Lomas swayed like a willow in the breeze.

I saw the hiccup under his robe as he reached his hand

into the holy water. His chest convulsed, and then a terrible guttural sound like muted thunder erupted from Lomas' chest as he spewed rivers of chewed walleye swirling in a pale red sauce right onto the child's head. Baby Maurice screamed louder, and the family leaped back in unison as if in a chorus line.

And then the dentist threw up, too.

EXODUS

I suppose there was an outside chance the substitution of holy regurgitation for water could have caught on and that a preacher with a missing eyebrow could have gotten past that impediment, but Fred Sturm was not in a forgiving mood. It had been a most inauspicious debut for young Maurice. The church council was convened two hours after the unusual baptism, and Lomas was driven from the temple. But there were parting gifts. A month's severance. And Tiny gave Lomas a ticket for not coming to a complete stop as he headed out of town the next day with all his possessions loaded in a horse trailer borrowed from a compassionate Methodist.

It happened right outside the Farmers Union Oil Co-operative. After someone hollered from the front, Irv dropped his wrench with a clatter and waved me along to the large glass windows in the front lobby. It was hard to find a spot among the gawking customers and the employees. Even Marv stopped his usual frowning and complaining from behind his desk to watch, bemused, as Tiny leaned his bulk against Lomas' aqua 1972 Chevy short box pickup.

Flies hovered around the horse trailer, which was still spattered with manure.

Martha did not come out of the office to watch. Outside, Lomas stared straight ahead behind a huge pair of sunglasses. In the office, Martha stared straight ahead at the wall, through her bangs, pretending to be oblivious to the commotion in the lobby.

Tiny inspected a burned-out taillight on the horse trailer while the red light twirled mockingly. We watched from the window, not gloating—just curious. That is when the BMW slunk in to the pumps.

When you work at the only gas station in town, you get to see a lot. You see them coming and going. Riding in high-and-mighty, slithering like worms to the gas pumps on the way out. Cars would roll across the black hose snaking across the driveway, triggering the bell that called me to pump their gas and to bear witness to the arrivals and retreats.

Irv started for the door, but I reached across his chest and blocked him.

"I'll get this one."

Diana was driving. Stanley sank a little lower in the passenger seat, hiding behind a pair of Ray-Bans. It was a cloudy day.

"Oh hi Diana," I chirped because I was so damn happy to see her. "Fill it up?"

"Yes, please," she said tersely. She did not look at me.

With the gas pumping ever so slowly, I grabbed the squeegee and sponge and began picking at nonexistent bugs on the passenger side of the windshield. "Hey, Stanley," I said through his open window, "I hear you're a heck of a fisherman!" He grunted and tried to smile, but it came off as more of an Elvis sneer.

I worked my way back to the other side. "So, Diana, what's new?"

Nothing much was new. Imagine. A high-society lady like that. Saints alive! I polished the windows for a long time. I had set the pump on the first notch so the gas was flowing at roughly the same rate the young Maurice was drooling in the backseat. When the pump finally clicked off, I topped it off to nine dollars even. Diana had the exact change. As I took the bills, she managed a smile, but I could see her looking past me at the flashing red light.

Though he was on the verge of writer's cramp, Tiny circled the Reverend Lomas K. Brown's pickup and trailer looking for other safety violations.

"Say, Diana . . ."

Her eyes darted back to mine.

"I just want to thank you for inviting me to the baptism." Her jaw got tight, and Stanley slid an inch lower in his seat as I continued. "I really enjoyed it. It was . . . *quaint*!"

The BMW's tires barked, leaving a black stripe on the driveway and the acrid smell of burnt rubber in the wind.

In the street, Tiny looked up at the infraction, shrugged, and then, satisfied that he'd written up everything he could squeeze onto one ticket, he waved Lomas away. The throng at the window dissolved. Irv and I walked to our cave in the back. Billy Preston's choppy piano chords rang from the radio. He's got a little story. . . . Ain't got no moral.

Irv started to bounce trying to catch the beat, which was always a prelude to the dance. This time I joined him. I twisted. I did the Swim. And the Hully Gully. We hopped about like grinning, drunken chickens with grease rags for tail feathers. It felt good to be alive.

Marv walked by and shook his head. He didn't complain like he might have most days that we were on the clock, and we sure as hell weren't the "goddamn Rockettes." But I was dancing pretty well. Diana Sturm Roberts did not know what she was missing.

An instant after the door to Pale Butte slammed behind Lomas K. Brown, another soul was sucked in to fill the vacuum. Exits and entrances—I saw them all.

The legend himself, Astor Malone, pulled up to the pumps two weeks later in a white Karmen Ghia. I knew who it was the minute I leaned into the window and saw the clerical collar and the face, too round for his trim frame. He was gray at the temples, but it was his shiny, bald head that clinched it. If you stood him beside the old pictures of the executives on the wall at the Third National Bank, he would have been a ringer for a younger Bull Malone.

I had never met Astor Malone, but his comings and goings, as he traipsed across the globe through the Peace

Corps and then on missions to other destinations with unpronounceable names, were dutifully recorded on the pages of the *Pale Butte Sentinel*. You have to keep track of anyone crazy enough to try to swim the floodwaters of the Sneaky River.

In recent years, the parish locales had been less exotic, and there had been many of them. Pastor Astor Malone was between churches again. You see, he had these ideas that stretched the boundaries of Christianity. You can see the Christian soldiers marching but keeping them all in step, now that's another thing. Martin Luther says it's one way. But the Pope can't be wrong. Joseph Smith says polygamy is all right, and Hugh Hefner agrees. Then God changes His mind, because He wants Utah to be a state. Politics are important to God.

And sports, too. *I'd like to thank my Lord and Savior Jesus Christ for giving me the strength to batter my opponent unconscious in the first round.*

Elizabeth Clare Prophet starts building bomb shelters in Montana and the government sends in tanks to deal with long-haired prophets in Texas. And you have the Astor Malones of the world. Square pegs and round holes, and we sit here trying to figure out the truth, if there is such a thing.

Pastor Astor Malone would come to towns from Mississippi to Ohio, from Wisconsin to Illinois, and charm the populace, rakish eyes twinkling, grinning like a child with a secret he can't wait to tell. Eventually, there were rumblings in the prominent pews where minds were buttoned down as tight as Sunday collars and sphincters tighter, where they are afraid to take God out of the box, hold Him up—or Her or It—and challenge the black and white and the cut and dried.

"Read between the lines," Astor would say. "Look inside. The answers to all the questions are already within you. Pull Jesus down from the pedestal and see that maybe the whole point of it all wasn't to become some unreachable icon. Maybe Jesus was the possibility—or even more, *the eventuality* for us all. Perfection awaits for us all in this lifetime or the next."

Maybe the Hindus, Buddhists, and Muslims won't go to hell after all.

Who knows about the Baptists?

"Perhaps," Astor would challenge his flock, abandoning the pulpit in midsermon, thinking aloud as he paced, ". . . perhaps *men* can turn water into wine, multiply fishes and loaves. And maybe," he would say, "just maybe, a man can walk on water."

That is what he would say. But because the difference between blasphemy and revelation can sometimes be hard to separate, he would be pushed along to another unsuspecting congregation desperate for a warm body. The cards would be shuffled again in the bishop's office to see where the joker would pop up next.

Fred Sturm made it clear from the start that Astor Malone was just pinch-hitting until a minister with an average vocabulary, two eyebrows, and a subdued libido could be found—preferably one who did not spend an undue amount of time on far-fetched interpretations of the scriptures or indulge in regurgitation-based baptismal rituals.

In the meantime, Astor was listed as "guest" preacher in the bulletin and on the sign outside the church. Because his stay was expected to be brief, Astor reclaimed his old room to the delight of Bull and Emily Malone instead of moving into the parsonage. The church council took advantage of the vacancy at the parsonage to gather volunteers to freshen up the paint inside and out and to repair the spongy wooden steps in the back.

As the parsonage took on a new luster so did the glow spread from Astor's smile. Mayor Bull Malone strode the sidewalks on Main Street like he had just won another landslide election, and Emily grasped Astor's arm and leaned against him as she led him on repetitive tours through every street, crack, and crevice of the town, stopping to reintroduce her son to the old-timers and to acquaint the younger ones with the heir to the Malone throne.

Nowhere was the prodigal son welcomed with more warmth than beside the shaman's boulder, at the feet of Joe Big Cloud down at the Sneaky River. I saw Joe's eyes sparkle many times. And I saw him smile on occasion, mostly around Coop and Maya and once in a while with me, but it was as if Joe had been rationing those smiles all along, and now they flew like sparrows gathering around the spilled grain at the elevator at harvest. Often, when I wandered down to the river to see Joe, Astor was there and sometimes Coop and Charlie

Brown, too, and you could hear laughter. And I swear that old snapping turtle was smiling, too.

One day, not long after he had hit town, Astor was dragged home by Coop for an unscheduled dinner appearance. It was not an unusual circumstance. Mom just waved him to a chair and sent me racing up to the store for another pound of hamburger before the door to Prunty's Store was locked at precisely 6 P.M.

After the obligatory twenty-minute chat about the weather and grain prices with my father, Astor stepped out to the backyard to watch me grill the burgers. We sat in the lawn chairs, moving them regularly as the smoke chased us in circular routes around the grill. Charlie Brown waited, ever the optimist, for a miscue that would send the meat tumbling within his grasp. He had not forgotten that Independence Day when I knocked six wieners off the steel bars. Charlie had liberated them from the grass below.

As Astor and I shuffled the chairs to dodge the uncanny smoke stalking us, we talked, the conversation driven mostly by Astor's questions and his squeaky voice. So we talked about this and that, about the way Tiny herded Spook back out of town and how he kept coming back scarier than ever. I told him about Joe and Charlie Brown's recovery, and Astor seemed interested but not surprised. When the conversation died for a moment, I rose to flip the patties while Astor and Charlie watched with equal interest and similar motives.

"Astor," I said, still half-wondering if I dared ask the question.

"Yes?"

"I've heard so many stories about the day Joe pulled you out of the river. . . ."

"Oh, that!" He grinned and leaned forward. "After all this time, people still talk about that?" He seemed pleased that we did.

"It comes up. The thing most of us can't seem to figure out is how Joe got to you."

Astor got a faraway look in his eyes and shook his head. "I wish I could remember," he said. "Oh, I have an idea. But Joe won't tell me how he did it."

I could see him re-creating the moments in his head, and I swear the visions began to leak out of his mind into mine.

"They say Joe brought you back from the dead."

"Oh, I don't know about that. It wasn't like that exactly. I remember floating . . . looking down and seeing my body and Joe leaning over me. And then, I swear he looked up where I was floating—*looked me right in the eye*—as if he could see me, and he told me, 'There is work to be done.'

"What I remember so clearly is that the words were in Lakota—*wowasi yustanpi kte lo*—but I understood. I understood like I had been speaking it all my life. And I know the decision to come back was mine, so I can't say that Joe brought me back from the dead, per se. But let's just say that Joe was mighty influential in my decision!" He laughed.

I moved the browning burgers around like checkers. "Astor, why did you jump in anyway? Was it suicide?"

Astor smiled wider. "Well, I never was an Einstein, you know. But no, it wasn't suicide. I never really thought I was going to die until I got sucked under. Then I was plenty concerned, but I don't recall ever actually processing the thought that I was going to die. Of course, what I learned is that there really isn't such a thing as death."

I stopped sliding the patties onto the platter and turned to look him in the eye, spatula suspended as I ignored the smoke in my eyes. Charlie Brown stared at him, too, cocking his head as if he understood every sentence. "You know this eternal life we've been striving to attain?" Astor winked. "It's already here."

LISTENING FOR MY HEART

I had to keep swapping the bowl from hand to hand as I carried it up the hill to Joe. It was still plenty hot. "Aiii!" I yelped, setting it down on the closest flat tombstone.

"Tuna casserole?" Joe guessed while I waved my hand in the breeze to cool the burn.

"Your favorite," I answered. "Complete with cracker crumbs on the top."

"Hmm," said Joe, lifting the aluminum foil. He reached into my shirt pocket to grab the plastic fork I had forgotten to give him. "You mother intends to make me a fat man."

I reached into my jacket pocket and set two fresh-baked dinner rolls down on the gleaming red granite tombstone. "Sorry. They're kind of smushed."

"Mgh," Joe grunted, his mouth full. He shrugged, which I took to mean I was forgiven.

I began idly reading the carved epitaph:

REBECCA A. COLLINS
JULY 12, 1920—AUGUST 16, 1959

"Spook's mother?"

Joe nodded, reaching for one of the rolls. The face of the stone had an extraordinary shine. The other tombstones were speckled with bird droppings. Most had green lichens clinging to them.

"You polish this one up special?" I asked.

"Nope. Every year for as long as I can remember, it always gets polished in July. It took me a while to figure out that it happens the night of her birthday; when I come up here the next morning the stone has been polished. I found an empty tin of Turtle Wax once. I think that's what he uses."

"Spook?"

"I think so."

"Odd."

"And every year, on August 16, on the anniversary of her death, he moves all the plastic flowers from the other graves to her grave. Takes most of a morning to move them all back."

Staring at that cold polished stone, for the first time ever, I considered my own mortality, and I got to thinking that if my lifeline was as short as Rebecca Collins' had been, I was more than halfway dead myself.

Facing death, it seems to me, is lot like having your

foot wedged in the railroad tracks. The sun is shining. There's no train in sight. So you sort of forget your situation. Hey, what's that over the horizon? Is that smoke? And I swear the rails are starting to vibrate a bit and . . . See? That's how it goes. Next thing you know, you're a goner, and you haven't accomplished squat.

The idea of being dead has never bothered me much. Dying, I can accept. Being smothered at the end by the weight of regrets, realizing you have not done what you could have done . . . lived the life you should have lived . . . I feared that.

Sometimes my life felt like Woof's Chevy must have felt as we circled the red scoria roads at night sipping suds or smoking Swisher Sweets. Aimlessly drifting. Sliding from second to third gear sometimes but always sliding back again to second, rarely hitting fourth, almost never hitting top end.

There had never been a plan, never been any real motivation. Not even enough to get on the waiting list for a union job at Halliday Steel in Boonesville where lifetimes were spent standing before long lines of presses and drills and calibration equipment making intricate gears for machines more sophisticated than their creators.

I convinced myself that I was comfortable, that there was still time to make my mark, but all that changed when Maya came into my life. Even as she breezed into my world, it felt like she was passing me by, like the whole world was passing me by, each soul a precise cog in the humming gears, sure of its destiny and its place. Suddenly, my eyes opened to a world bigger than I had considered, and I started to feel small and overwhelmed and, worst of all, directionless.

"You know, sometimes I feel like I'm wasting my time here," I said to Joe as I looked down across the river where Coop was trimming the last unruly hairs of the park lawn, completing the circuit he would begin again in three days. "Everyone seems to be going somewhere, doing important things, making big money, and I don't even have a plan."

He thought about that for a moment.

"Everyone has a plan," he said. "Some hide from it. Others lack the courage to act on their destiny. Many do not recognize the opportunity. In the meantime, are you really wasting your time here with me? Are you wasting time in those moments you spend with Coop, your parents, and your friends?"

"It's just that here everything seems to move so slow. And yet I feel like my life is rushing past."

Joe nodded. "I have been to the big cities," he said. "I have seen the people scurrying back and forth, and they are working to have moments like this. They strive to build up bank accounts. They seek to purchase memories and moments. They seek the things you have."

"So this is it for me? Just another grease monkey in a podunk west river town?"

"Ah, Bones, your journey will take care of itself. Even now you are moving. Look at the river. Sometimes it appears calm. Sometimes it boils and rushes away and frightens us as it carries us along. Sometimes it seeps. Other times it floods. The water always finds a means to flow.

"You will learn to understand when you have slipped from the flow as easily as the fish does when it is beached. You may try to swim upstream, but eventually, even the most subtle current will win, and it will carry you where you must go."

As I remember those words, I do not know if I grasped them then. I have traveled countless roads, and the journeys have been many since that day. But now I see the greatest distance traveled has been within. I still get impatient sometimes. But then my impatience was worse.

"It's just that I feel inadequate. I see classmates come back. It's like they're evolving, and I'm just scraping my knuckles on spark plugs. I feel like I need to be out in the real world!"

"Do not be swayed by the illusion when you see your old friends return in new suits with thick wallets and shiny cars," Joe said. "Ask yourself why they have returned. What is it they seek back here?"

"I dunno. I always figured they came back to rub it in."

Joe shrugged and managed a thin smile. "You already have what they want to rediscover. The trick is not to let your head lead your heart. Have you ever made a decision with your heart and found it to be wrong?"

I thought about it. "No."

"That is because it is not possible."

"So how do you tell if it is your head or your heart that is speaking?"

"Your head speaks loudly like a drunkard. Your heart whispers."

I started to walk in silence down the hill. I listened for the quiet voice, but the din of thoughts in my head overwhelmed all else, and I could not hear my heart.

Speak up, dammit!

ANOTHER PATH

That night, we were at Joe's and for once the turntable was not spinning. As we noisily barged through the door, Butch's boots clunking and Maya giggling at another wry observation from Woof, the crackle of voices came from Joe's kitchen radio. Leonard Peltier had been sentenced for the murder of two feds on the Pine Ridge Reservation, and now there was talk of an appeal. Joe silenced our chatter with a slow wave. And then we listened to the news.

The whole American Indian Movement standoff in 1975 had been unsettling for us South Dakotans. Actual *news* didn't happen in South Dakota, and except for watching George McGovern get massacred by Nixon in '72, the national press didn't know where South Dakota was, much less give a damn. Half of them think Mount Rushmore is in *North* Dakota. But give a handful of braided brown men rifles, surround them by the lily-white FBI agents in suits and sunglasses, and "Boys, we've got a story out there in the sticks among the hicks."

We were used to watching Walter Cronkite deliver the news, and it always came from somewhere else. News didn't happen *here*. It happened in Vietnam. We watched it nightly as our boys ducked in the deep grass and fired bursts at an enemy that may or may not have been there.

We saw the bodies. We saw flies circling the emaciated bodies of skeletal Biafran children while pork chops fried in our kitchens. Jimi Hendrix died. Then Jim Morrison and Jim Croce. And in Ireland they fought and died over religion. Nixon went to China. Angela Davis stood defiant in an Afro crown. Palestinians killed Israelis at the Munich Olympics. Fischer beat Spassky.

Oh, we saw the news all right. Picasso took a dirt nap, but Peter Max lives. We could see the riots in Watts; there was Watergate and Patty Hearst.

We knew there was danger out there. *Out there.* We sent our boys off to Da Nang and sometimes we got a coffin in return. Some headed off to Denver and one ended up dead after a repossession gone bad at Five Points. But the danger was always out there—out of reach. It was something you had to seek out. It was not something that visited the open prairies. Foolishly, we believed we were immune. Then for the first time, we started to see that ugliness and uncertainty in our midst. We half-expected a bunch of well-armed, pissed-off Indians to kick down our doors in the night.

"You can't blame them for fighting back," Maya said. "We've taken everything from them."

"I didn't take nothin'," Butch said, leaning back, tilting his white cowboy hat to reveal a windburned face and a peeling nose. "That fight was between my great-grandparents and their great-grandparents."

"But don't we owe them something? We took the country from the Indians and then we built half of it on slave labor. And now blacks and Indians are living in poverty. And I don't care what you want to say about things being equal. They're not!"

Woof smiled a wan apolitical smile, scrunching his eyes beneath his mop. "I think you're gonna fit in just fine at Berkeley," he said. "You might want to look up Jane Fonda."

"It's Stanford, you turd," she said, her pointed chin jutting forward. "Joe, what do *you* think?"

I remember shifting uneasily. You sure wouldn't want to ask a real live Indian about the plight of real live Indians, would you? I did not expect Joe to answer, but he did. That was Maya's gift. The rules of engagement, of social decorum, and I think at times, even the precise orbits of the planets would have suspended at her command. Even now, I wonder what happened. How did she do it?

I think of the mystic hypnotized, the chanter of chants, the miracle man falling victim to the spells of a seventeen-year-old beauty. She was still a bit gangly like a colt, but every bit as formidable as any wizard or any prairie shaman. The beauty of the gift was that she seemed so oblivious to it. But how could you know that every room you entered was transformed by your presence? How could she know that for the rest of us, the world did not sparkle and shine the way it did for her? How could you expect her to know that the glow of the room came and left with her?

"Peltier is a warrior," Joe said. "And warriors accord themselves differently in battle. Some rise. Some shrink. Some kill because they hate. Others kill, and it is justified. I do not know what the truth is here."

"The bottom line is two FBI agents are dead," Butch said. "They finished them off at point-blank range. Ain't nothing noble in that."

"It is unfortunate," Joe said. "It is also unfortunate that the reaction is punished, while the actions that preceded it are not. If you are slowly being strangled, as your air is cut off, will you not fight desperately? Will you not do anything to survive?"

I think Butch remembered how it felt.

"This is how I see it," Joe said. "When the settlers came and then the soldiers, they did not understand the Indian way, so they dismissed us as ignorant and as pagan. Slowly, with white schools and white books they choked off our connection to the Great Mystery. A soul knows when it is not right with God. So it struggles. Sometimes it struggles unwisely. All it understands is it is being choked off. It begins thrashing about. It does desperate things. When you fall so far away from God the journey back may take lifetimes."

"What if that never happens?" Maya asked. "Then you just burn in hell forever?"

"I do not believe that," Joe said. "We will all find our way back to God. That is our destiny."

"So you don't believe in Judgment Day?" Maya asked.

"In the end, each man must judge himself. When this life is over, the spirit will measure the deeds. If a man has not been righteous, he must amend that in the next life. If he has things to learn, he must study them. If he owes debts, he must pay them."

"My minister says you only live once and then you either go to heaven or hell."

"Perhaps the interpretation is incomplete. Or incorrect."

"So you don't agree with the Church?"

"It is a path. All paths lead to God. Of course, some have more detours than others!" He chuckled, his laugh rolling softly like a warm breeze through a cold room. "Christianity is a path. Buddhism is a path. The Lakota way is a path. Our ways are old, and our knowledge is ancient. We understand that great civilizations have risen and fallen. It causes us to be humble and more respectful of Mother Earth's wisdom. This civilization with our cars and televisions is not the greatest and not the wisest the world has known.

"Worlds have come and gone and a new world awaits. You are young enough that you may live to see this rebirth. Mother Earth will cleanse herself, and then there will be a new world—the Fifth World. The Hopi, the Navajo, and the Mayas know this to be true. This wisdom has been passed along from grandfather to father to son. Prophecies have been made and fulfilled, so why should we not believe these things we know to be true? But this truth has been dismissed by the white man."

"What about Jesus?" Maya asked. "Don't you believe in him?"

"The Lakota saw the truth in the white man's religion," Joe said. "We recognized that Jesus was a holy man. But our ways and our holy men were not given respect. We all worship the same power. Does it matter what our name for Him is? Yahweh. The Great Mystery. Jehovah. Krishna. Buddha. Wakan Tanka. God. Allah. The Lakota have known Him since the beginning. He was not introduced to us by the white man."

Joe leaned forward and looked around the room at each one of us.

"Do you think that the miracles Jesus performed were the only miracles ever performed? I have seen great medicine men materialize eagle feathers from thin air. I have seen terrible illnesses cured. Tibetan monks can create a ghost servant simply by wishing it to be. We live in such darkness," Joe continued, his voice building. "I do not believe miracles are miracles at all. I believe they are as usual as the sunrise each morning and the sunset each evening. But we are like children, and we do not understand. No, we are less than children! A child does not believe in the impossible. He is taught to doubt. Doubt itself is a disease, and we are all infected.

"We travel many trails before we reach heaven. We live many lives, and we must experience many things before we have evolved. So in this life, I am Lakota. But perhaps in another life I was a white man. Before then, perhaps I was Chinese or Japanese. We all are one people. We are sparks from the same light. In the end we must all be rejoined."

ELVIS HAS LEFT
THE DRUGSTORE

The kisses had gotten longer, more urgent, and though we both refused to talk about it, Maya's time in Pale Butte was rushing away like water through a sieve. There was desperation in the kisses, and even when we had stopped to catch our breath, we searched one another's eyes.

I let myself believe that she would be back in my arms in the end. I was not sure how the plot would roll out, but I let myself believe that love would find a way. She would grind her pelvis against mine, and my hands would grip her from behind to pull her closer. She was mine if I wanted her, and I have never wanted anything quite so much. I regret not giving in to the urgency. I think about it. I wish I had possessed her. I did the right thing, I think. Sometimes I wish I had not.

One afternoon we sat on the bench in front of Prunty's Store dining on Velveeta and hard salami sandwiches she had brought me for lunch. We avoided any conversation about the few days left before she would leave.

"You'll make a fine little housewife someday," I said as I munched away. She frowned at my teasing. "Yup. Mopping floors. Changing diapers . . ." She grimaced. "Ladies Aid meetings on Wednesday night . . . PTA on Thursdays . . ." I continued. "Casseroles made with tomato soup and a husband who will clip his toenails in the recliner at night."

She was horrified. "That's not what I'm all about!"

"Sure, you and Gloria Steinem are gonna change the world." She punched me hard on the arm. It left a bruise. She was distracted when the door to the drugstore eased open, and Spook stepped out wearing a brand-new pair of rose-colored sunglasses.

"Check it out," Maya said.

"Uhh, huh."

"Elvis has left the drugstore," she said.

Spook stared at us, especially at Maya, as if he knew her from somewhere else. We watched as he walked west. I took another bite, chewing mechanically as I pondered the meaning of the fashion statement. Spook's couture had never varied much from worn dress pants handed down from his old man and shirts with buttoned-down collars. Sometimes the pants were plaid and the shirts paisley, a clash so severe it threatened to trigger passing epileptics. And now, rose-colored glasses.

"What's his story?" Maya asked. "Was he ever normal?"

"Normal? Hmmm. I don't suppose he was ever *normal*. Maybe as cat assassins go, he's normal."

"What's he got against cats?"

"Search me. His old man has a Manx he just dotes on. You can see him staring out the window, and that cat is always in his lap. He buys cases of tuna for that cat. I doubt he treats Spook that good."

"I kind of feel sorry for him."

"I used to," I said. "But not after what he did to Coop. And there was that thing with Ginger Leesburg and after that, the Douglas girl."

Spook continued to shrink in the distance as he plodded toward the edge of town.

"Does he ever talk?" Maya asked.

"I've never heard him. I guess he just shut down after his mother died."

"I heard it was suicide."

"Well, Spook's old man wasn't convicted. But well-insured people have a history of dropping dead around him. And when the old man gets low on cash the next time, Spook's gonna wake up dead, too."

"You can't blame Spook for being the way he is, then."

"I don't blame a shark for being a shark, either. But I still know he'll eat me if he has the notion."

FIREWORKS

That night Butch made it to town in his torch red 1965 GMC pickup before Woof showed up at my door. I answered the banging at 9:30, and when I flung the door open, Butch tilted his white straw "town hat" back good-naturedly, revealing the scar on his ear. Norm had done a pretty fair job of stitching, so the scar wasn't bad at all. I still found myself looking for it, amazed at the way this thick-necked wrangler had settled into our lives like he had always been there.

I would catch myself inspecting the back of his head from the backseat as Maya and I tilted against each other, the way the skin of his neck rolled under close-cropped brown hair when he kicked his head back to laugh. I was searching for the intimidator, I suppose, wondering where he had gone.

"Quit lollygagging," Butch said. "Let's go for a ride. And bring that good-lookin' little heifer with you." Maya pouted, unsure if being called a good-lookin' heifer was really a compliment at all. Butch steered toward Woof's home with the dated dark green asphalt siding. Tanya came to the door before Butch could knock. "You got a warrant?" she asked.

He grinned. "Tell Woof to give up. We got the place surrounded."

Now she smiled. "He's not back yet."

"On the lam?"

"I wouldn't put it past him. But he said he was going to the junkyard to scout for Chevy parts. Rear end's going out on the Chevy again."

"Some alibi."

She smiled some more and Butch grinned back.

"So, uh, you wanna come out for a drive in my limousine?"

"What about Woof?"

"Well, you're better lookin' than he is."

"Smarter, too," she said. "Wait here." She checked on Rose and then reemerged a few minutes later, hair freshly combed, a hint of makeup, and a floral blouse draping over her swollen belly.

Four's a crowd in a pickup cab, especially when one is eight months pregnant. Butch rattled around in the pickup bed, sliding aside his work saddle, lucky green lariat, sledgehammer, and other various paraphernalia of the ranching trade. He draped a clean gunnysack over a spool of barbwire, hoisted Tanya over the end gate, and motioned her to sit. She eased down and he leaned against the cab, steadying her as I drove, lurching along, until I got used to the clutch.

"Hey, Butch," Maya yelled over the chugging of the motor. The cowboy's eyes were riveted on Tanya Schwartz. "Butch . . . BUTCH!"

"Huh?"

"You got anything in here besides George Jones?" Maya asked rifling through his eight-track case.

"Got some Tammy Wynette in the glove compartment."

"Hick."

"Thank you."

George Jones it was. I adjusted the mirror as we drove, spying on the passengers in back. I caught only snippets of conversation and an occasional giggle. The coy smiles spoke volumes. I tried to be subtle about it, but I would swerve suddenly around the turns as we puttered on the back roads, flinging Tanya toward Butch, who gallantly steadied her. As he held her in rough-hewn hands, it was obvious he was becoming putty in hers.

When we drove back to town, we swooped into Woof's yard, but he did not appear at the door. Tanya and Butch were still busy flirting in back, so I went in to get Woof. The spring slammed the dried-out wood of the screen door loudly behind me. Nothing.

"Anyone home?" Nothing. "HEY, WOOF!" Nothing. I walked past the flowers on the wall in the dining room and headed into the living room. I heard the soft drone of the television. Rose was lying on the couch, sleeping, buried under a puffy quilt although it was oppressively warm. Her painfully thin face rested on Woof's lap. He was dirty and darkly tanned, so it was hard to separate the grime from his brown skin. He was sleeping hard, head tilted back.

I stood there for a moment, the voyeur, and I followed the lines on Rose's face under the wispy, dry, graying hair. The lines framed her nose, looping gently over her cheeks, connecting under her lips. Above the sofa was a portrait of Rose, Woof, and Tanya taken in easier times. She had been a handsome woman. I stood there for a while lost in thought. As I walked out, I couldn't get my eyes to focus.

George Jones was singing, "It's been a good year for the roses. . . ."

"Are you okay?" Maya asked when I slid back into the driver's seat.

"I'm fine," I said, staring straight ahead.

"Where's Woof?"

"Sleeping. Out like a light."

But *I* didn't get much sleep that night. The fire whistle howled at 3 A.M. At first, I thought it was a dream, and when I awoke, the whistle was fading. The trucks were pulling away from the fire hall by the time I got there, so I ran the five blocks to Tiny's house. I was winded by the time I got there. Five blocks!

The Rambler, parked outside the door to his modest house, was in flames.

Joe was already rolling out the hose from the Mack truck, so I veered to the old Studebaker to help. Grumpy Mindeman opened the door to the cab and promptly fell out.

"You gesh the hosh and make ish snasshy," Grumpy ordered to his crew, which pretty much consisted of me.

"Goddamn!" Tiny spat as he stepped toward us, draped in a ridiculous long nightshirt, his hair sprouting at odd angles, looking like an oversized unkempt ghost. Joe and Bull already had the hose out, soaking down the car and the overhanging box elder tree. If the tree caught fire, flames could leap from tree to tree and take out the block. Or worse.

Tiny began rolling the hose off the Studebaker, and I fired up the pump.

That's when the shooting began. There was a bang. And then another. And then I heard the sound of a slug tumbling past my ear.

"Incoming!" Grumpy hollered, ducking behind the truck beside me, Tiny, Bull, and Marty Leesburg. There was a cacophony of bangs and pops.

"What the hell?" Bull said.

We pasted ourselves against the truck and listened, trying to figure out the sniper's location. He appeared to be shooting from *inside* the flaming passenger compartment of the Rambler.

"Fuck!" said Tiny.

"What?" Bull asked.

"That's my ammo going off!"

"How much you got in there?" Bull shouted over the thump of 12-gauge shells and the crack of .45 Magnum cartridges.

"A shitload!" Tiny answered.

"Fuck!" said Bull as a slug whirled crazily past. Without a gun barrel to concentrate the energy and the direction of the bullets you wouldn't think exploding ammo could really kill anyone. But there wasn't a one of us willing to test that theory, so we huddled there, pinned down by one hell of a fireworks display. Joe peeked over the back of the truck with the hose, dousing the tree as best he could without having his ass shot off. That's when the Rambler's gas tank exploded.

You know how you see those car explosions in the movies, and there's a ridiculous orange ball of flame and parts fly, and you walk out of the theater complaining about how fakey it all was?

It was exactly like that.

"Holy shish!" Grumpy said as the *woosh* of hot air enveloped us.

The hood landed on Gunnar Smithers' house. Some newspaperman. He slept through the whole thing. But other than that and the spot on the street where the asphalt had melted, burned, and bubbled, the neighborhood was intact.

"That son of a bitch," Tiny cursed, drawing the words out over five or six extra syllables. "That crazy son of a bitch!"

"What?" I said. "Who?"

"He's settling scores. That's what. You think it's a coincidence that Bertram Sumpter's house burned down, too? That crazy motherfucker has finally gone completely fucking nuts. Jesus, Mary, Joseph, and all the Jews!"

"That Spoosh needs hish ballsh cut!" Grumpy said.

"Shit. Grumpy, how much have you had to drink?" Tiny asked.

"A couple," Grumpy figured. He swayed like cattails in the breeze.

"Sweet Jesus! And they let you behind the wheel! Bones, what the hell is the matter with you?"

"But . . ." I stammered.

"I ain't that drunt," Grumpy argued.

"Oh yeah!" Tiny said. "Let's hear you recite the alphabet."

Grumpy got stumped on R.

He thought about it for a long time but couldn't come up with the next one. Then he shook his head. "That's a sad reflection on our educational shystem, ain't it?" he said.

That really set Tiny off. When he tired of Tiny's rant, Grumpy snapped that he wouldn't have gotten so "drunt" if he had known there was going to be a fire.

The feds, the county sheriff, the highway patrol, and the state fire marshal were in town the next morning. The fire marshal concluded that the Rambler "had blowed up," which, of course, made it official.

Spook had an alibi. He was home the whole time, his old man said, grinning with those black teeth. "Call my lawyer if you got a problem with that," he told Tiny. "You know the number."

IT GETS HOTTER

Two nights later, it happened again. The fire whistle moaned, and I jumped up from the couch and the embrace so quickly, my teeth scraped Maya's mouth, and before we were out the door, her upper lip was swelling and pouting even more at the interruption.

She followed as I sprinted the two blocks to the fire station. The real race was not to get to the fire but to see who would get to the "good truck"—the 1959 Mack fire truck—and who would be stuck with the 1947 Studebaker M15, which topped out at about forty-five miles per hour and required all means of double-clutching just to approach that speed.

Joe drove the Mack out the door with Bull and Grumpy Mindeman on back and I could see my father was riding shotgun. That left the Studebaker to me, Gus Martell, his cane, and Woof. We did not need to ask where we were going. We could see the smoke billowing.

Sarah Leesburg was enraged. Joe had to stop her from

entering the trailer house again to retrieve what she could. Five kittens stumbled underfoot mewling as hoses drenched the tin. The water boiled like spit on a hot iron. Sarah had saved the television and the eight-by-ten photo taken the day she got to shake Winston Churchill's hand. But everything else was gone.

Sarah might not have made it out if she hadn't fallen asleep on the couch. The bedroom had gone up in a burst of flames first and anyone sleeping there would surely have been trapped. Marty had ended up working a double shift at Halliday Steel in Boonesville; otherwise, he might not have made it out, either.

Sarah was mad as hell as she tried to recruit anyone who would listen to lynch Spook, who leaned against a tree across the street in the shadows, watching the flames lick the branches of a tall box elder tree leaning over the trailer.

"You know goddamn well it's that fookin' loonitic that dun it!"

She tugged my sleeve. "You know he dun it, right?"

"Well . . ."

"Don't no one see? He's gone starkers. Ye know he's watchin' that sweetie of yours, too."

"Well . . ."

"Don't you see, Bones? Don't you see she's the spittin' image of my Ginger when she was a child? When Spook . . . *Don't you see?*"

The fire marshal was never able to say for sure that it was arson that caused Bertram Sumpter's home to burn down, but Tiny's car was a no-brainer, and before the ashes of the Leesburgs' modest pile of belongings had stopped smoking, the fire marshal was convinced that the fire had been helped along by one of Marty's gas cans out back.

Of course, Spook had nothing to do with it, his lawyer said, and Tiny came out of Josh Rustan's state's attorney's office red-faced, because he wanted to lock up Spook.

"You need evidence," Josh said. "You have to follow proper procedure."

Sarah Leesburg wanted "that mootha fooker's testicles dangling from me rearview mirror!" She even tried to circulate a petition, handwritten on a scorched yellow legal pad, to have Spook run out of town permanently, presumably after he had been transformed into a eunuch. Ella signed. My parents and Coop signed. And Coop signed for Charlie Brown. Butch signed. Woof, Maya, and I did, too.

Everyone else just walked away from Sarah and her pen, afraid of Spook. Afraid of his old man. Afraid of his lawyer. When Sarah handed the pen to Joe, he waved it away, too, but not because he was scared. He recognized it for what it was, an impotent scribble of ink on a sheet of paper.

The idea of a petition seems quaint to me now, but it is entirely typical of small towns in the Dakotas. Petitions are constructed, bereft of any legal weight, to have those damn kids stop playing their car stereos too loud or to have that slutty Trixie Johnson stop wearing so much perfume or on any number of inconsequential and inane topics. The petitions are dragged to city councils or school boards where the elected ones somberly study the documents, huddle, and agree that yes, this sure is a petition all right, and a whole lot of people know how to write their names, and by golly, we sure do have a crisis on our hands. And then, the petition gets filed away like the Rosetta Stone for a couple hundred centuries while the board or council agrees to remain concerned about the issue.

In time, when Marty was able to laugh about the losses, he noted that Sarah had not seen fit to rescue their wedding portrait, which had hung right beside the glowering Churchill. But his biggest complaint was that she had not saved his accordion.

"Well, every cloud has a silver lining," a neighbor would invariably crack.

That fall, the boys at the VFW raffled off a custom-built ice shack with a propane heater and an antenna that could pull in *both* television stations, and that raised enough money to replace the Leesburg home with a used but nicer trailer.

Now as I look back, it seems so obvious that things were coming to a head. And Joe knew it, too. "The time comes when you have to cull the herd," he said.

VISION QUEST

I do not know if I am typical or by nature a coward, but I know that for the longest time I dodged confrontation. I steered away from the wall. I played it safe. But you know what?

Trouble found me just the same.

It sniffed me out like a bloodhound.

It stalked me.

I lowered my head and tried to appear nonchalant. Still, trouble found me, vulnerable and ill prepared, the way teachers had in math class as I stared at the incomprehensible squiggles wondering how A and B could somehow equal the square root of 16 and how the alphabet ever got involved in algebra in the first place.

Trouble always found me. Always, as I slogged away, in slow-motion nightmares, looking over my shoulder, hiding in hedges, I hoped that this time, oh God, please, I could avoid the confrontation.

Somewhere along the line—I do not remember

when—I realized that when you spot trouble on the horizon and you know it has spotted you, it is easier to move toward it.

The waiting is far worse than the actual event. Now, I see a confrontation and I don't like it, but I move forward to meet it. I do not embrace it.

Guys like Joe Big Cloud have that figured out from birth. But just when all hell was breaking loose around us, while smoke and steam still wafted from charred heaps in Sarah Leesburg's yard, while Spook was planning who knows what next, Joe decided to leave town.

It wasn't the first time Joe had disappeared for a week, telling no one but Mayor Bull Malone. We had always speculated that he was visiting family down on the Rosebud Reservation or maybe at Pine Ridge, but we never knew for sure, and it was something you didn't ask. We didn't know for sure if Joe had family beyond a dead mother and if he did, where they were. It was as if he threw up this almost visible barrier at times, keeping the queries at bay.

Joe had unwritten rules. Children seemed to know instinctively the times they could frolic around the river, scare the fish, and chatter nonstop to a bemused Joe. And there were other times, indiscernible to the eye, but as tangible as the boulder on which he sat, that Joe repelled the incursions, questions, and disruptions.

I do not know if the rules were less obvious to Maya or if she chose to ignore them or if they simply did not apply to her. But time and time again she would probe and almost always Joe would share at that moment that which he had chosen not to share in three previous decades in Pale Butte.

One night not long after the Leesburg fire, we barged in and found Joe carefully rolling a change of clothes into a horse blanket. Joe cinched the bedroll tight with a belt and placed it at the door beside his medicine bundle, which was a hard leather pouch bound by three leather shoestrings. An old army canteen wrapped in camouflage canvas lay on the floor beside the other luggage.

"Hey, handsome man, you running out on your gal?" Maya teased.

Joe shrugged but did not smile like he usually did for her. "I'll be back."

But she continued to stare at him and it was clear she wanted an explanation.

Joe sighed. He walked to the couch, and Maya followed. She sat between Butch and Joe, holding Joe's hand. Joe waved Woof and me to our usual positions at the table, and we settled in for the interrogation.

Catholics visit the Vatican. Muslims trek to Mecca. The Lakota journey to Bear Butte. *Mato Paha*, as it is called in Lakota, rises twelve hundred feet above the surrounding plain a few miles northeast of Sturgis. Sitting Bull and Crazy Horse walked this mountain in search of holy visions. Custer trampled through seeking gold. And now Joe Big Cloud would return.

"Why?" Maya asked.

"To prepare," he said.

"For what?"

"I . . . don't know. But it's coming. Something's coming."

For three or four and sometimes five days, they sit cold and hungry and thirsty, waiting for the sacred visions. In time, the pines may start to whisper and the meadowlarks begin to speak. "That is where I had my first vision," Joe said. "I was eleven. Then the vision came to me again in other years. Each time it was stronger."

"What did you see?" Maya asked.

Joe paused a very long time as he replayed the vision in his head.

"This place. The river. The turtle. Eventually, I knew I must find this place. It was difficult. I did not wish to leave my home. There was a woman I would have married. But the vision persisted. So I came."

"So what is it you're supposed to be doing here?" Woof asked.

"I suppose it is what we are all here to do. To learn something. Maybe to teach something. But not all has been revealed."

"Did you ever wonder if maybe God gave you the wrong directions?" Woof asked. Butch snorted an embarrassing loud honk through his nose in an effort to stifle the laugh. Maya elbowed him, but even Joe had to smile.

You had to wonder. Pale Butte is a blip on the map, a lot of nothing in the middle of nowhere. You'd like to think that if God is going to send the disciples out, He'd at least be smart enough to send them somewhere where there are more people than cows to get the message.

"Well, there were times when I thought that myself," Joe said. "I suppose there's a fine line between a vision and hallucination. But along the way, there are signs that tell me the vision is real and that I am where I am supposed to be. Things in my vision have come to pass."

"So you know what's going to happen in the future?" Maya asked.

Joe pondered the question. "I hope not. It's difficult to sort through what could happen and what's absolute destiny. I think God gives us a little wiggle room here and there to change things for the worse or the better. After a while, though, it all seems to get jumbled up in my mind, and I can't tell what is coming from my imagination and what is coming from the vision. Sometimes I don't know what to believe, my faith wavers, and I start to wonder if I'm crazy."

"How do you know you ain't?" Butch asked. He got another elbow in the ribs.

"Oh, I wonder. But like I said, there are signs. Farmers keep bringing me sick animals, and they keep getting better. That reminds me that there is something at work here. But sometimes that isn't enough, and I start to confuse the signs with coincidence, and I have to renew the vision. But when I walk off that mountain, I leave my doubts and fears behind."

I had never imagined that Joe Big Cloud could have doubts and fears. He just seemed so *certain*. As for me, I always felt like a hiker lost in the woods. Everywhere I turned there was another tree, another doubt, another fear. So this idea of depositing my doubts and fears up on a big pile of volcanic rock seemed pretty appealing.

My own visions could sure use some sorting out. All I could see was a bewildering blur of long-legged redheads riding away on buses, drooling old dogs, Edsels crashing, and that damned Spook staring from every shadow. I wondered if I might leave my nightmares on the mountain and walk away. It made four days on Bear Butte without food and water sound pretty good.

"Joe," I said, and then just as quickly regretted opening my mouth. But by then everyone was looking at me, so I had to finish. If I could have thought of something else to say, I would have. "I was wondering if you'd mind if I tagged along."

If Maya could have reached me, she would have elbowed me. The gall! Intruding on the visions of a holy man. *Oh, so you're going to speak with God, huh, Joe? Sure, why don't I come along? Me and God go way back.*

And of course, there was so little time for us.

Joe considered the request.

Then he looked at me for a very long time.

And nodded.

Marv gave me holy hell for wanting a week off with less than a day's notice, and Maya nearly stopped speaking to me, limiting her responses to grim, terse *yeses* and *nos*. Her time in Pale Butte was short, and now I wanted to use some of that precious time to go on some macho camping trip in the Black Hills.

I had a duffel bag over my shoulder at 5:45 the next morning when I knocked at Joe's door. I had grown tired of waiting. The sun was only a glow in the east. My sneakers were damp from the dew. The crickets chirped. I had waited, drumming my fingers on my table at home. Then, I had grown impatient. Then concerned.

I knocked again.

No answer. The bus would be here in twenty minutes. I assumed we would ride the bus.

The door was unlocked. I peered in. The bedroll was missing and Joe Big Cloud was gone. I heard the mournful whistle of the train chugging up the rise to the trestle. It was headed south.

Marv was already scowling into the dark recesses under a car hood when I walked up at precisely 8 A.M. in my work clothes with my air pressure gauge in my pocket. He scowled and kept digging and cursing the elusive plug.

"Well?" he snarled.

"I cut the trip short," I said. "I guess I missed your sunny disposition."

He set the ratchet on the air cleaner with a clank, wiped his hands, and fired the grease rag at me. It hit me in the chest, and I caught it as it rolled slowly down my shirt. Marv stalked away, still muttering about the undependability of kids today and how hard it is to get good help and son of a bitch, those dumb bastards at Dodge must have spent weeks finding the most goddamn inconvenient place to stash that fuckin' eighth spark plug.

"How 'bout me? Did you miss me?" the sultry voice taunted. I turned to see Martha in the shortest of skirts and a crisp, white blouse, the top two buttons undone, revealing a glimpse of tan cleavage. Like every man would for the rest of the day, I looked at her, starting at the ankles, sliding up the tan and the curves to those penetrating eyes. Good God, you could kill someone dressed like that. She waited patiently for my eyes to work their way up to hers.

"You new around here?" I asked.

She pretended to huff, but she had to bite her lip to keep from smiling.

THE DREAM

Two nights after Joe left me behind I had the dream. I call it a dream, but it was more than that. To call it a dream is to suggest that it was not real—that I was not swept out of my bed into another time and another place. The maddening thing about the revelation—and I recognized that it was exactly that—*a revelation*—the maddening thing was, I did not understand at the time what was being revealed.

The obvious answer is, I am mad! It means nothing. But no madman in his right mind could be considered any sort of decent madman if he admitted his madness.

If you discern the madness, it ceases to become madness. It becomes more of quirk, an eccentricity, a curious little aside in the conversations that preface your introduction to a friend of a friend. *"Let me introduce you to Bones. He's a good guy. But let me warn you, he ain't quite right in the head."*

It was in the Rocky Mountains. That is where I found myself in the dream. To the west the mountains were violet, blocking the setting sun. I was with Joe Big Cloud, and we stood at the edge of the deep valley, rich and lush with grass. He did not speak, nor did I, but we stood gazing down into the valley where a prim ranch was cradled near the bottom. The trim, white clapboard house glowed from the light of a kitchen window, yielding enough light to outline a red barn and surrounding corral. I was struck by the neatness of the ranch, nestled in among modest scrub scratching out of the incline.

Joe's arm extended, pointing out over the ranch so that in our silence, there would be no mistake that this is what he intended me to see.

I was struck by the intensity of the wind from the north. It was a furious wind, unlike any I have experienced, and I have seen big blows. I have cowered and gripped the walls of culverts to keep from being sucked out by tornadoes twirling rubbish, cows and cars overhead in a prairie sky. I have been knocked flat by bully blizzards shoving snow to the south. But this wind was beyond a wind. It howled through what I perceived to be my astral body, yet it could not move me. Nor could it wash away the home hiding in the divine crease. Above, in the maelstrom, a menagerie of debris streaked by as if flung by a disgusted, petulant god-child.

Though the wind could not dislodge me as I stood there, the awful howling created an ache. I ached for warmth, for the womb where I might be protected from this tumult.

That is when I saw my mother walking in from the

northwest, impervious to the wind as Joe and I were. She was older in the vision. Her hair was silver, pulled back in a simple bun, and though her face was that of a grandmother, it was smoother now. She smiled a comforting smile, unconcerned at the thrashing of the earth, exuding the same sense of calm that had soothed Coop and me in the crises of youth.

In her arms was her knitting, flowing behind her like a bridal train, and for the first time, the many colors that had seemed to me to be so haphazard appeared to merge before my eyes into a precise design that I was finally able to fathom. Imagine staring at a blue period Picasso for years, and then one day, an epiphany is delivered, not explainable with mere consonants and vowels. You look at the brushstrokes, and for an instant you are transported into Picasso's brain, and you witness from behind his eyes what is flowing out.

Mother tenderly wrapped my ethereal body with the ethereal blanket. The ends were free from the loose strings that Charlie Brown had unraveled over the years.

"It is finished," my mother said, as the earth boiled around us.

So we stood there, Joe to my left, my mother to my right, as the storm blew through us and rattled the earth like a coyote shakes a cottontail.

In the west—*the west*—the mountains began to glow. Joe lowered his hand and we turned to watch as the sun reappeared and moved swiftly *backward* across the sky. The wind tripled in fury and swept the earth like a righteous broom. Trees were bent flat to the ground, roots exposed for a moment before they were washed away in a shrieking sea of dust. Others were splintered in sawdust explosions. The short scrub pines that remained rooted were stripped of needles.

And then it was quiet. Eerily quiet except for the shrapnel raining down from above. Weathered planks fluttered down, discarded by the sky like so many feathers. In the valley, now littered with smatterings of this and that, the ranch remained.

Whatever this was, this was not the end of the world. There was incomprehensible devastation, but the sense I have of the moment is strangely neutral even as I sensed a rush of newly released souls swooping past like the wind itself.

This was not the end.

It was a beginning.

A transformation.

Suddenly, I was tumbling away. The ranch was gone and so was my mother. I was transported to a place I knew to be Bear Butte, though I had never been there before. I was standing at the edge of a campfire that had settled down into embers. I stood inhaling the smoke. It was sweet with sage. In the glow was Joe, sitting, eyes closed and cross-legged in a meditative reverie like a Trappist monk. Dozens of red ribbons were tied in the trees around the fire.

Yet, there beside me, seeing his physical self as clearly

as I, was Joe. His arm extended, sweeping past his own sil-
houette at the fire and out over the towering black pines in
the dusk and to the valley in the south, framed by the soft
dark velvet of the Black Hills. I strained to see what he was
showing me.

I leaned into the night.

To awaken from a nightmare is a relief.

To awaken from a dream such as this was tragic.

Now, I have seen a glimpse of what Stephen Hawking
must have felt in those later years when he was wedged in a
wheelchair, separated from the world by his withered body.
What dreams he must have dreamed. Oh, to whiz through
the universe in your dreams and to understand, to perceive,
to have it all make sense . . . and then, to awaken in the
chair, imprisoned, to *realize* and not be able to tell.

For men like Hawking, the end is not the end. It is liberation. Don't you see? Even as you talk and walk and run
and see and smile, you are not free. You are simply able to
move your prison. But the bars are there.

Damn, the bars are still there.

HE WAS DELIGHTED

A couple days later, Tanya Schwartz came to me with a problem I had been trying to ignore. "Bones . . . Bones . . . Bones . . ."

I don't know how long she had been standing there while I sprinkled sawdust on the concrete floor to soak up the oil by the hoist.

"Bones!!!" I looked up to see the now-painfully pregnant Tanya, hands on hips, harrumphing at me in jest.

"Oh, sorry, Tanya. Guess I'm a little brain-dead this morning. Got a lot on my mind."

She scanned the blot of oil soaking into the sawdust compound. There was the clank of a hammer as Irv pounded on the side of an old Ford tractor in the next bay. The air compressor's electric motor whirred. Slowly, the smile slid from Tanya's face, and she looked wearier than a sixteen-year-old should. I sprinkled the last of the sawdust.

"It's Momma. . . ." Tears flowed. One, then another,

plopped onto the concrete. "She's not eating. And she can't walk without leaning on me."

"She'll bounce back," I said. "She's a strong woman. She just needs some time."

"What she needs is to go to the hospital!" Tanya snapped. "But she's too stubborn to go. She says if she does, she won't come out again."

"Can't Woof talk to her?"

She sobbed. I reached to console her, but she jerked back from my embrace. "I'm okay," she said, sighing. "Bones, he just doesn't seem to get it. He just acts like nothing's wrong."

"He gets it."

"Then why doesn't he show it? Bones, when Woof's around, Momma pretends like she's just fine. She smiles and she laughs at his stupid wisecracks. And he just acts like everything's finer than frog's hair. Like nothing's going to change. *But everything is going to change!* It's like one big lie. I'm the only one who knows the truth . . . the whole shitty truth!" She cried some more, and this time she leaned against my chest.

I held my arms away from Tanya's back to keep the grease on my arms and hands from staining her blouse. She pulled closer, crying harder. I could feel her swollen belly pressing against me. Finally, I gave in and wrapped my dirty arms around her. In time, she pulled back, letting her arms slowly slide down my back until they were free. I lowered my arms, too, pulling the ever-present grease rag from my back pocket, using the cleanest end to dab her tears. Each dab left a little grease smear. The more I tried to clean the smears, the more I smeared. She laughed. "Bones, you are hopeless!"

"Yeah, I majored in hopeless and minored in pathetic."

She laughed again. Then the smile faded, and she looked at me with a little tilt of her head. For the first time, I did not see her as the silly, grubby little kid that interrupted her big brother's games and conversations.

"You'll talk to Woof?"

I did not answer.

"You're the only one he'll listen to," she said.

"Tanya, Woof never once listened to me."

A smile creased her rounded cheeks under puffy eyes. "He listens. He needs you more than he lets on. He just doesn't want to give you the satisfaction of *knowing* he listens. Tell him Momma needs to go to the hospital," she said. "Tell him she will go if she hears it from him."

I stood silent. I could not commit. Her eyes implored me.

"I . . . I'll try," I said, and then I paused, wondering if I should say what I wanted to say. I said it anyway. "Tan, your mother is right. If she goes in, she won't come out."

"Yes, I . . . I . . ." She could not finish.

The conversation weighed on me that day, and when Maya brought me sandwiches for lunch, I was too glum to eat. But by suppertime I was ravenous. I was still sawing on my second pork chop when Mom untied her apron. Dad was pushing away from the table. Before he could rise, she plopped into his lap.

"Hey, sailor!"

"Geez, Olivia, that hurts! A guy's lap can only take so much," he said.

"Are you suggesting I've lost my girlish figure?" Mom asked.

I dropped my fork with a clatter. "C'mon, Coop," I said. "Let's go for a walk." I waved him to the door, and he did not argue. Mom blew into my father's ear. Coop leaned back to see what was transpiring past the doorway. I grabbed him by the scruff of the neck and pulled him out.

There are things you don't want to know. One of them is how hot dogs are made and the other is that your parents had sex. When I learned about fornication and procreation on the playground—*it was just hearsay, mind you*—I was forced to consider that my parents actually engaged in such things. I avoided the thought for a considerable time. Years, in fact. But ultimately, I conceded that the event had happened. Twice. No more and no less. And I am sure they did not enjoy it.

Coop and I played kick the can for blocks until Coop stubbed his toe. We discovered two dead cats along the way, both lying with fangs bared and flies buzzing about the corpses. Charlie Brown sniffed with interest. "Do you think Spook killed them?" Coop asked as we leaned over the second one. I thought about telling him they'd been hit by cars.

"Yeah, I'm afraid so, slugger."

Coop meditated on this for a while. "Why does Spook do bad things?"

"I dunno," I said. "I guess so many bad things have happened to him, he wants to make everyone feel bad, too."

"Sometimes I feel bad for him," Coop said.

"Geez, why, Coop? He almost killed you!"

"I feel bad because he's different. I know what it feels like to be different."

"Coop, you're not different," I said. "You're special. That's why everyone loves you."

"Maybe if someone loved Spook, he would be nice."

"He had someone once," I said. "His mother loved him the way your mother loves you. I think he misses her a great deal. He polishes her tombstone on her birthday. And every August sixteenth, he puts flowers on her grave.

"Why every August sixteenth?"

"That's the anniversary of the day Spook's daddy killed her."

"He killed her? Why did he kill her?"

"Because he's a bastard."

"Maybe that's why Spook is mean."

"Could be."

"I would get mean if my momma died."

"No, Coop. I don't think it is in your heart to get mean. You would get sad. Very, very sad."

I couldn't help but think about Rose Schwartz and

Woof and Tanya and what they were going through. As I considered just how to approach Woof as I had promised Tanya I would, it struck me that as close as I felt to him I did not remember a time when we had ever had a serious discussion about *anything*.

There had been serious times, but mostly we endured them in silence. I was there for him and he was there for me and that was enough. There's a stoicism that permeates the prairie soil and the air. It's not that we don't feel anything. It's just that we won't *admit* that we feel anything.

Eventually Coop's feet and mine led us to the river. I don't suppose I have ever wandered out for a walk in Pale Butte that didn't end at the river. It was just so peaceful there. Joe was there, just back from his pilgrimage to the Black Hills, and he was oddly buoyant, so I didn't want to break the mood by complaining about being left behind.

"Hey, boys!" Joe called as we approached, and it startled me. Always before, I had initiated the conversations. I had always been the one to reach out, to peal away the onionskin layers.

"Hey," Coop said. "Catchin' anything?"

"Bullheads, mostly. But I'm really not up for cleaning them, so I've been tossing them back."

"We found two dead cats," Coop told Joe, switching conversational gears as his mind shifted from one thing to another. "Spook killed them. His dad's a bastard."

Joe opened his mouth to reply but stopped. Coop was already on to the next thing, poking a stick into the mud.

Coop dug his stick in deep at the water's edge and watched the water slowly seep in. Charlie Brown lapped water from the river, startling a small school of minnows. They darted away in choreographed unison.

Coop came shuffling back. "Here, Joe. I found this rock for you."

Joe took the piece of flint, which was rounded by the passing water, and solemnly placed it in his shirt pocket. "Thank you, Coop. It is a wonderful gift."

"Yeah. I'll be getting lots of gifts myself in a few weeks. For my birthday."

Joe nodded.

"I hope I get a skateboard."

"Coop, I don't know if that's such a good . . ." I said.

"Wouldn't you like a skateboard, Joe?" Coop asked.

"Sure," said Joe.

I frowned at Joe. He shrugged an apology.

We stood in silence a while longer until he began packing his tackle box, a signal that our visit was complete. I rose to leave. Charlie Brown stretched, and I waved Coop along. I was climbing the embankment when I heard Joe's voice behind me.

"Bones, did you enjoy your first trip to the mountains?"

I turned to look at him. He stretched out his arm, pointing into the distance, posing as he had in the dream. And he grinned a toothy grin, eyes shining.

He was delighted.

BEWARE DISTORTIONS
OF THE TRUTH

I don't think I slept that night, and the idea that Joe and I had walked through the same dream distracted me all through the next day. When Coop and Charlie Brown wandered into the lobby at 4:30 the next afternoon, I punched out early. We found Joe at the river.

"Joe, how did we have the same dream?" I asked.

Joe set his rod down after a precise cast. Charlie yelped joyfully behind us as he and Coop wrestled in the grass.

"It wasn't a dream," Joe said. "I said I would take you with me, and I did."

We paused as the rumble of Ella Peterson's rapidly accelerating Sting Ray approached and then passed. The engine whined as she streaked up the hill.

"It felt like the end of the world."

"Lomas Brown would have called it the Apocalypse," he said. "The great medicine man, Wovoka, called it the

Purification. And that is what it is. When you are unclean, you wash. Mother Earth will cleanse herself. It has happened before. It will happen again."

"What do you mean?"

"Look. What do you see? You see buttes and trees and grass and the river on a dead ball of mud. I see life. The rocks are alive. The earth is alive. If everything is comprised of atoms in constant motion how can they not be alive? The earth is alive, and we are poisoning her. Even the most docile animal will fight back when endangered."

I wonder if the fleas on a dog view themselves the way man does himself, as a civilized society, relentlessly expanding territory under the charter of their own Manifest Destiny, believing that when the hind leg rises up to scratch a few dozen away it is something akin to a volcano at Pompeii. Even now, when a mudslide buries a thousand here or an earthquake swallows a small city there, I imagine a cosmic hind leg swooshing down, brushing the infestation away.

"We have forgotten how to communicate with nature," Joe said. "We have forgotten how to nurture our Mother Earth. Even among my people, there is only now a reawakening to this knowledge. The Purification is an awakening. We have been malicious children sleepwalking. Even now, eyes are fluttering open. There are some who understand the grave path we are on. They are awakening, and now they are trying to shake others awake as Wovoka did."

"Who was this Wovoka?"

"He was the first Ghost Dancer. That was long ago. He was a Paviotso medicine man in Nevada. He grew up with a white family and they taught him about Jesus. So he learned that Jesus was a great healer and that he could command the elements. He knew Christ could quiet the storms and turn water into wine.

"Wovoka believed. Then a powerful vision came to him during an eclipse. He saw God and those who had passed into spirit long ago, and he was given a message. It is the same message all churches teach one way or another.

"People must be good.

"They must love one another.

"They must not fight.

"They must not steal.

"They must not lie.

"And Wovoka was granted a view of the future, just as you have had the privilege. The earth will become cleansed. The old ways will return. Game will be abundant once again. Bellies will be full.

"Wovoka believed the Ghost Dance would bring this Purification sooner. For the sick and starving Lakota at Wounded Knee, it was a message of hope. Many embraced it. So the Ghost Dance swept into the prairies. But it began to frighten the whites, and they tried to stop it. This unrest is what led to the death of Sitting Bull and the massacre of so many at Wounded Knee."

"I don't understand. Why would it frighten the whites?"

"Like all religion, it got distorted. There were those

who did not embrace Wovoka's commandment that they must not fight the whites. A few began to believe they should take it upon themselves to punish the whites. Such is the arrogance of man. He begins to believe that he must do God's work for Him.

"But what frightened the whites most was that the Ghost Dance brought the people hope. A people with hope are a formidable people. You must understand. The whites sought order and assimilation. The missionaries came in and began to wipe out the old beliefs on the reservations. They were certain they were doing God's work.

"The reality is that there are many pieces of the truth. It is better for us to search for the pieces and to assemble them. But when a fragment of the truth is shoved forth as the whole truth, there is arrogance in that. Any belief that one fragment is superior to another will cause anger. There is anger from those who are subjugated. And when they rise up, there is anger from oppressors because they cannot accept the challenge to their particular truth. If anger and violence grow from a belief, you can be certain it is flawed. So it was at Wounded Knee."

I tried to imagine what took place that winter day in 1890. By some accounts, two hundred ninety Lakota died that day. The Ghost Dance died with them. Some thirty-three soldiers fell, too, most the victims of friendly fire. The survivors got medals.

Some years later, I was drawn to Wounded Knee on the centennial of the massacre. I went to honor the dead and the living and those in between. Mostly, I went for Joe. Even after a hundred years, in the morning when the December cold turns your lungs to ice and the early morning wind is just a bitter whisper, if you listen long enough, if you listen close, you will hear the screams. The screaming of slaughtered children echoes forever in my mind.

"Beware distortions of the truth," Joe said. "Beware of arrogance."

Suddenly, his reel shrieked, and Joe swept it to his hands. He was not fast enough. The line snapped and the monofilament drifted back in delicate curls on the surface. Whatever it was disappeared with the hook. The moment punctuated, we sat for a long while staring at the calm river.

"Sometimes I do the Ghost Dance, and I sing the Ghost Song," Joe offered. "My grandfather taught me in secret. He would take me to the hills, away from the others, because the Ghost Dance was forbidden. Grandfather told me I must not dance for destruction. I must dance for rebirth. I must dance so the dream may live. When he was too old to dance, Grandfather gave me his Ghost Shirt. He said I must share the secret of the dance with my son. And I must teach my son to heal." A very sad look came to his eyes. "Grandfather believed he was the last Ghost Dancer. If that is so, now I am the last."

I did not know what to say to that. You know, you stumble along in this life, believing one thing, and then you wake from your dream to discover that your dreams are real, and it causes you to wonder if maybe your daytime hours are the illusion. You wonder if you've been clinging to the wrong reality.

I started wrestling with that the moment I realized Joe and I had shared the same dream. Then, when I became convinced we had not shared a dream but a reality, it made my head swim. I wondered if my mother had really been in the dream or if her presence had been some sort of metaphor. Anything is possible in dreams. I wondered if she was sorting through the dream like I was but was afraid to talk about it, because everyone knows that anyone who puts much credence into dreams is a wacko. Or a licensed therapist.

In the dreams there were no limitations. The sun could rise from the west if it wanted to. It took me years to get comfortable with the notion that dreams could be real. The anxiety the notion provoked was simple. If dreams were real and not an escape from life itself, then there is no way of avoiding life and one's purpose.

You are irreversibly immersed in life.

In my teenage years, I railed at the injustices of being young and not in control. I raged at my parents and my circumstance. I was furious. Resentful. "I did not ask to be born!" I shouted, lashing out at no one in particular and lashing out at everyone.

One day, not long after the summer of '77 was a memory, I remember sitting in contemplation early one Sunday morning on Joe's boulder. I had risen before the sun because I could not sleep. On those occasions when my mind dashes away from the dream world and balks at going back, I do not toss and turn and fight the awakening, because it does no good. I rise.

With morning's glow causing low-slung cirrus clouds to radiate from below in a marvelous maroon, I strolled, hearing the first sleepy songs of sluggish birds, the comforting chirp of the crickets, the rattle of beetles' wings, and the gurgle of amorous frogs. As always, I was drawn to the river.

I considered the things I had learned and tried to sort out the meaning of it all. I thought about the circular motion of life. We spiral, hopefully upward, and not as if circling a hellish drain. We live. We improve. And we choose to come back to school for another lesson.

We choose.

We choose.

I imagined floating in the heavens and spotting my father and my mother, below with a beautiful young boy. I saw them from above, gently, gently and joyfully caressing Coop. And my soul ached to share that kind of love. I imagined, and it seemed so real that perhaps it is a true memory, that I had decided at that moment to join them.

I believe that is what happened.

In the moment that realization appeared in my mind, it was as if a bedroom window shade had whirred open and illuminated the dimness. My frustration melted, and my resentment followed, because, you see, I had chosen to be here after all. And if the decision was mine, well then, *that* was different.

Suddenly, life didn't seem quite so oppressive. I may have looked around some days and still concluded that I was mired in one deep, ugly frustrating place. But when you realize that you are responsible for your own karmic circumstance, and that there is no one else to blame for it, it is a liberation. You realize you can't play dodgeball with the universe. You can't hide in your dreams.

You can't cheat life.

"Life is not fair," the pessimists tell disillusioned children to explain newly discovered tragedies. But they are wrong. Life is inherently fair.

We may chafe under the karmic justice because we do not perceive the karmic offense that preceded it. And sometimes, many times, there is grace. God intercedes and gives us a get-out-of-jail-free card. So we get plenty of breaks. If you consider that, life is not only fair, it is more than fair.

A thought, a realization, can change everything. I chose to be here, and so did you. Mystics might call it a revelation or enlightenment or an epiphany. But to me, it just felt like waking up. Your eyes feel the light, even though they are closed. You throw back the cool cotton sheets, sling your legs over the side, and you stretch. Things move slowly for a while. You may be stiff and your mind still a bit dull. You may stub your toe. You may yawn and fight the urge to return to your burrow under the covers.

But then you hear the early birds chirping. They are

already on the job. And now it is time for you to get to work as well, you decide.

You decide.

You decide.

DEATH IS ALWAYS EASY

Before the summer had even ended, I could feel our Gang of Four coming apart. We could all feel it. Even as Maya and I clung desperately to each other, we knew she would be pulled away. First home to Jersey to pack for college and for the perfunctory good-byes with old friends. And then she would be gone, probably forever.

Woof began working part-time gigs at a radio station in Boonesville. He was awfully good from the start, and I envied his bravado.

Even Butch was pulling in a new direction. I don't know if I believe in love at first sight and all that soul mate stuff, but if there ever was a case, it was Butch and Tanya. There was a magic there that even an old skeptic like me can see. She was there when Butch needed her, and I know it was quite a revelation for Butch the day he realized he needed anyone at all.

I don't believe it was coincidence that he was there when she needed him most.

It was August 16, 1977. I remember it was the day Elvis died, and you wouldn't figure things could get worse than that. Butch was dropping off Tanya after a picnic at Dry Lake when they saw the smoke and someone who looked a lot like Spook lurking in the hayfield at the edge of town. The first floor of the Schwartz home was engulfed and orange tongues lapped the inside of the windows like ravenous dogs.

Tanya jumped out before the pickup had stopped rolling and fell because her legs could not accelerate fast enough. But she leaped up instantly on bloodied knees and dashed up the steps to the front door. Racing behind her, Butch caught her by the ankle as she shoved the kitchen door open. He pulled her back just in time. Flames exploded outward, rushing to the oxygen, and singed her hair as he pulled her away screaming.

Meanwhile, Woof and I were changing a tire on a gravel road in the country as Maya watched. As we finished, Woof saw something in the distance. "Looks like smoke." He lowered the jack, and the yellow Chevy eased back down. "We'd better go in," he said. As we got closer we could see the smoke billowing from Woof's end of town. He crushed the accelerator, and we careened down the dirt road shortcut.

We were too late.

The neighbors walked away, heads down, shuffling away like druids from a funeral. The departing throng split as we roared into the yard, not speaking a word. Sagging, somber faces did not need to speak. They glanced up at us and then back down at the ground.

Butch held Tanya tight as they watched the glow of the embers collapsing into the cement basement. Woof ran through the crowd, seeing the looks but not wanting to believe them. His eyes searched, looking for a ninety-pound wisp of a woman draped by a threadbare housedress, four sizes too big. When he found Tanya, one anguished look from her told him everything, but he had to hear it.

"Momma?"

"She's gone."

They said she hadn't suffered. The end came quickly, they said, in a rush of hot air and smoke, instantly searing lungs and spinning Rose Iris Schwartz into unconsciousness. That is what the experts always tell the survivors.

They do not suffer when the car rolls over them in the ditch after nineteen beers and two shots of Jack Daniel's for the road. They do not suffer when they fall from the water tower on Halloween night. They do not suffer from the cancer or the heart attack or the stroke. When the space shuttle explodes, they do not suffer. When the swimmer disappears beneath the waves, he does not suffer. When the broker loses it all and stuffs a .38 caliber slug into his ear, he does not suffer.

Death is always easy.

Even though they are not dead, the experts know these things.

Be comforted.

This isn't going to hurt a bit.

I collapsed. I dropped the phone and collapsed the day I lost *my* mother. I could not breathe as an overwhelming sense of desperation smothered me. I knew—*just knew*—if I refused to believe it, it would not have to be true. But Wolfgang Schwartz did not collapse. He did not cry that day. He *glared* at the flames. He held Tanya tight, and then he took her chin in his hands and whispered something that caused her chin to stop trembling. Her jaw stiffened, like his, in resolve, and they stood at attention until Sela Rosemount tottered up and wrapped her arms around Tanya. Butch drove them to Sela's home in his pickup.

When at long last Woof turned to look at me, I dropped Maya's hand and walked to him. "Woof . . ." I said, but I could not finish before the lump in my throat swelled, and I began to sob, weeping for both of us, because he could not cry. He would not give them the satisfaction. He put his arm around me tenderly and smiled a hint of a smile. "It's all right," he said. "It's all right, buddy."

I tried to compose myself, because that is the way west river men are supposed to face devastation, stoically with brave, noble smiles. The buttes are watching. We must be oblivious to heartache because to recognize the wound might mean dying from it. Why weep over tragedies? The sun and the moon have witnessed far worse than this. There is always something worse, we tell ourselves in consolation, and we thank God for going easy on us.

"You can bunk at my place, Woof," I said stupidly with snot seeping from my nostrils.

"Yeah."

"Door's always open."

"Yeah. Thanks."

"Just take what you need for clothes."

"Thanks, Bones."

He stared at the smoke. "She deserved better," he said. "Her life was too hard. Too goddamn hard."

"She didn't think so, Woof. She had Tanya and you. She was proud of you."

"I should have done better."

"You did your best, Woof."

"Not always."

"You did plenty," I said. "You've been a good son. The best."

I left him there with soot on his face. I turned to leave, stepping on a bouquet of plucked and wilting dandelions. As I walked away with Maya, over the crackling and popping of the charred wood, I heard him speak softly to the smoke.

"Momma, I'm sorry. I am so sorry. . . ."

He seemed to sag under the weight of it all.

I realized then that Tiny was right. Spook *was* settling scores. I wondered if he would come after Coop again. And then I remembered what Sarah Leesburg had said.

THE ASTOR MALONE
TREATMENT

I inhaled and savored the rush of a cool, fresh morning breeze sailing through my open window. For a moment I was relieved. Morning. Maybe it had just been a bad dream.

I dropped my feet onto the floor and pulled the hair out of the creases of my squinting eyes. My hair was definitely getting long. Too long, I knew, but I let it grow past my shoulders, a message to my father that he did not rule my follicles any longer. I never looked good in long hair, but that wasn't the point. My head was a battleground ruled by coaches and my father and the disapproving *tsk-tsks* of the church ladies. They planted flags on my head like marines on Iwo Jima, like Roald Amundsen at the South Pole, claiming it as their own.

It's a hair revolution, baby.

My hair smelled like smoke.

I had never seen so many people milling about in the Farmers Union station. I heard a low murmur from the front as I walked through the side door to start my shift. As I poured my first cup of coffee from behind the candy counter, I watched Tiny clatter by in the city work truck, which had been called into double duty as a police car.

"What gives?" I asked Martha.

"The town is crawling with cops," she said. "I hear the FBI is coming, too. Tiny went to haul Spook in last night and he wasn't there."

Then she leaned closer and I could smell a sweet hint of jasmine.

"Bones, that's not all. . . ." She was whispering though it was apparent to me that every single person in the lobby knew what she was about to tell me. "When Tiny searched the house, old man Collins was missing, too. They finally found him. Dead. In the freezer."

The coroner's best guess was that Ernest Collins Sr. had been dead for several days, considering the decomposition of the half-eaten burrito on the TV tray in the living room and the other half, partially digested in the wizened old freak's gullet.

It was not the burrito that killed him, though in the beginning it was a prime suspect. Until they discovered the handle of a six-inch Phillips screwdriver jutting from the corpse's left ear.

The old man's hands were folded in his lap the way undertakers arrange them, and a bouquet of thirteen dandelions lay on his chest. His prize Manx cat lay beside him.

Pale Butte went nearly seventy years without a murder if you don't count Spook's left-handed mother committing right-handed suicide or her daughter succumbing to crib death at the age of nine. Now, Tiny had two corpses, a missing suspect, a shitload of paperwork, the attorney general screaming at him through the phone, and a scorched piece of blacktop outside his house where his Rambler police car had been officially "blowed up."

Astor Malone delivered one heck of a eulogy at Rose Schwartz's funeral. He amplified the traits of Rose Schwartz to such an extent and made us feel so good that such a woman had known and loved us, I suspect that some of the older ladies in the congregation couldn't wait to rush home and die so they could get the Astor Malone treatment.

Don't get me wrong. Rose Schwartz was a fine woman, a great woman, but she had her flaws. For one thing, she drew her lines in permanent black marker. Once you wronged her, you remained exiled from her life. And she swore like a sailor. I went into shock in the third grade and did not come out of it for two days when I heard her direct a string of expletives at her husband that could make foul-mouthed gas station managers look like pikers.

I do not wish to speak ill of the dead. It's just that I get uncomfortable with putting dead people up on pedestals just because they're dead. Hell, everybody dies. I swear if some preacher starts blowing smoke up the congregation's asses about what a near-perfect human being I was, I will sit bolt upright in the coffin, red-faced and embarrassed, and I'll tell you now, that will ruin a perfectly good funeral.

Woof shoveled the first spade of dirt into Rose Iris Schwartz's grave. The sun amplified the greenish bruise on his cheek. He'd gotten falling down drunk the night his mother died and couldn't remember exactly how it had happened. He passed the handle to Tanya. Sobbing gently, she wriggled free of Butch's arm and scooped a pile of pale brown clay.

Joe shook Woof's hand after the service, holding it for a long time. Butch shook Woof's hand, too—with his left hand. Two fingers on his right were splinted together after being bashed against a fence by a cow.

I looked around at the sorry sight we had become and wondered when we had stopped being invincible.

Coop gave Woof a big hug. "Everything is going to be all right," he said. Bull and Emily Malone sent the biggest bouquet, and Emily cried the hardest.

Woof had no idea what the funeral would cost. I do know Woof was surprised that such a magnificent brass and mahogany casket, and later a massive black granite stone, could be had for less than five hundred dollars. *Rose Iris Schwartz*, it read. *Born March 19, 1933. Died August 16, 1977. Too quickly did the bloom fade.*

Woof realized in time that he had had some help with the funeral expenses. Many years later, when the day came for Emily Malone's funeral, he saw to it that there were a thousand yellow roses for her in the church. When he saw them, Bull Malone broke down.

No one came to the funeral of Spook's father. The

feds about drove Tiny bat shit crazy, demanding he turn the town upside down and find the fugitive Spook. It was uncomfortable for folks, not knowing where Spook was and if he would return. It was even worse, in some respects, than when he was stalking the alleys.

Soldiers I knew who came back from Vietnam told me how some slowly went insane, hacking through the brush, waiting for a sniper to end it all or for a foot to trip the booby trap. It's easier when you see the enemy, a battalion in black pajamas bearing down on you in an open field, AK-47s spitting brass. There's a certain perverse comfort in knowing you are screwed. At least you know.

GRUDGE AGAINST JACKRABBIT LINES

Lefty Schlosser said after the PTO shaft on the tractor snagged his sleeve and ripped his right arm off at the elbow, long after the stump healed, it still would ache and itch sometimes like the arm was still there. But an empty, pinned-up sleeve was all he had to see to convince him that things had changed, the loss was real, and things would never go back to the way they were.

As that summer wound down, I got downright agitated when I saw the Jackrabbit bus pull up to load and unload passengers across from the Farmers Union station. The driver would drop off a package of some car parts we didn't have in stock, three or four times a week. He was a nice enough guy, but without really thinking about it, I began getting surly when he breezed in with a quick Ole and Lena joke that had everyone else laughing. I stopped laughing at his jokes because I saw him for what he was—the enemy. He and that bus were going to take Maya away.

I don't know if she ever understood how hard it was for me. I know it was hard for her.

"Bones," she said, "you know in the beginning I didn't want to come here this summer. I was so angry. I was sure I was going to end up in gingham dresses that look like table-cloths at some barn dance with a bunch of hayseeds. I did not want to leave New Jersey."

She held both of my hands in hers.

"Now my friends back home don't seem so important," she continued. "I'm half afraid they're going to seem shallow to me. When I get back there, I'm afraid I will have outgrown them. I feel like I've changed."

"How so?"

"Well, back home, everyone looked at me as just an-other dumb teenager. My parents. My friends. Here, every-one treated me like *a person*. I don't know how to explain it, but with you, I became someone . . . *better* than I was before."

I was floored. It had never dawned on me that some-how I had inspired her.

I did not allow my eyes to wander from her face. I wanted to savor the moments, to imbed them in my mem-ory. That is one of the gifts Maya left me that summer—the understanding that everything—*everything*—is of a transi-tory nature. A brief flicker, and then it is gone.

As a parent, you may begin to understand the pre-ciousness of the sacred moments. Your children swirl past you and leave you spinning, and if you aren't careful, they will leave you dizzy and unaware that something special is here and disappearing in the same instant.

Life streaks by like a Vida Blue heater.

She wrapped her arms around me. She held on for minutes. The kisses got more tender in those last days. Almost sorrowful. Her lips would gently close around my bottom lip, pulling it, and when it slipped away, her lips would return.

"I don't want to go," she said.

"I'm going to miss you," I said, in perhaps the largest understatement of my life.

"Oh, Bones!" She paused, frustrated. A bit angry. "I love you," she almost snapped, peeved that she must admit it. Then she said it again, the way it should be spoken. Tenderly.

"I love you."

I kissed her cheeks. Her forehead. Her chin and finally, her lips. "It's funny," I said. "I try, but I can't remember a time I didn't love you. It's as if I've always loved you, and all it took was seeing you on that bike that day to remind me."

She caressed my hair, weaving her fingers, like a comb, through a tangle.

"I never understood why you picked me. Woof always gets the girls."

"Woof didn't look at me the way you did."

The gang had one more night together though we almost had to pry Butch away from Tanya with a crowbar. He hovered at Sela's home while Tanya mourned for her mother. "I just don't feel good, leaving her alone like that," he said. He stared at his hands. "I just think she feels better when I'm around," he said finally. "And the baby's coming due and . . ."

"I get it," I said. "You don't have to explain. But I'm glad we can get the gang together one more time before Maya leaves. It wouldn't be the same without you."

Parked just off a section line at the squishy edge of a pond, we laughed, drank a little beer, and listened to the Guess Who through thin-sounding, tinny speakers.

No time left for you,
On my way to better things...

I leaned over to kiss Maya as we leaned back against Woof's Chevy, and for once I was not self-conscious about Butch and Woof looking on. When I leaned against her to the wail of Randy Bachman's guitar, I spilled some beer on Maya's tight jeans.

"Hey!" she shrieked at the cold shock. And she splashed me back, right on the chin, which got Woof and Butch grinning.

So I splashed them. "How funny is it now?"

Apparently it was hilarious, because Woof and Butch tackled me and began dousing me. Maya came to my rescue and began drenching Woof and Butch.

We giggled and wrestled and splashed. It was the fastest we ever went through a case of beer. When all the ammunition had been expended, we stood with matted hair, stinking like barflies, and wrapped our arms around each other as if in a football huddle. The shrieks subsided in time to laughs and the laughs into giggles and grins and the grins into smiles. And then the smiles faded, too, as each one of us realized that change was upon us and that nothing would ever be the same.

We stopped at Joe's so Maya could say good-bye. A flea-bitten coonhound with a splinted leg bayed mournfully at us when we knocked. Joe raised an eyebrow at our stench and our unkempt, sticky hair, but he did not criticize. He just smiled the same sort of wistful smile we were smiling and spread newspapers on the couch for us to sit on. We did not stay long but long enough for Joe to drop the needle on Sinatra for one last dance.

"So now you are going to fly away," Joe chided gently as the last notes disappeared into the night and his arm fell away from Maya's hip. "Now I will have to find another to dance with me."

"That would be lovely, I think," she whispered, her eyes welling.

"It's no good, dancing alone," Joe said.

He cupped her chin in his hand and looked at her. She wiped at her eyes.

"Good-bye, handsome," she said.

She threw her arms around Butch when we dropped him off, hugging his neck tightly. "I'll miss you, cowboy," she told him.

Butch nodded. "It's going to be quieter around here without you," he said, his voice cracking a bit.

"You take good care of Tanya."

"You take good care of *yourself.*"

Woof shut off the engine when he dropped Maya and me off at my place. He stared ahead until Maya reached over and gently turned his head toward her. His sticky hair was trimmed short from the funeral.

"If you ever want to dump that loser," he said, tilting his head at me, "you know who to call."

"I'll keep that in mind. You know I was using him to get to you, don't you?"

"I figured it was something like that," he said. He leaned over to kiss her on the forehead. "Maya-girl, you made me smile. There were times I wasn't sure I remembered how to smile. Especially lately. But you always made me smile."

"So that is my legacy?"

"It is." And he smiled the saddest smile I have ever seen.

That was the end of that marvelous Gang of Four. In that moment, we began gently unraveling the way a beautiful woman unwinds her braids, sitting before the mirror at the end of the day.

Maya and I were silent as we climbed the stairs to my apartment in the glow of a forty-watt bulb. There was only the creaking of the stairs and then the squeak of the door, which announced our arrival to no one. It already felt lonely inside and she wasn't even gone yet.

She kissed me lightly and stepped into the bathroom.

"Oh, God! Look at me!"

I rushed in. She stood under the harsh flickering of fluorescent light. Her hair was clumped. Her face was sticky and streaked with dirt.

She was perfect.

"I'll draw you a bath," I said. "And you can rinse out your clothes in the sink." I started the water running in the claw-foot tub. The pipes clanked and shuddered. She turned away from the mirror and kissed me sadly and I kissed her back, sadder still. Then she stepped back and slowly began unbuttoning her blouse. With a shrug, it fell to the cold linoleum floor, and her bra followed, exposing small plump breasts, lightly freckled, with tiny pink nipples. She pulled my hand to her chest and I kneaded the hot flesh, our eyes riveted. Then her hand dropped to her flat stomach and began unbuttoning her jeans. I kissed her breasts while her jeans crumpled to the floor and her panties followed.

We embraced there while the water flowed and steam began to settle like dew on the fixtures. The misted mirror obscured the image of our embrace. When I broke our embrace to turn the spigot closed, she lightly touched my arm.

"You could use a good scrubbing, too," she said.

I did not sleep that night. I lay awake and watched her sleep, and even though my arm went numb, I refused to move it from beneath her head. Her jeans dried stiff as planks on the brass-colored radiators, which hissed and rattled.

Her grandmother was beside herself in the morning when she discovered Maya's bed had not been slept in. When Maya walked in with me to toss the rest of her things into her suitcase, she glared at me. I stooped to carry Maya's suitcase the two blocks to the bus stop.

"It's not his fault, Grandma," Maya said.

Bertha glared some more.

Coop and Charlie Brown were waiting at the bus stop with an obscenely large bouquet that must have taken out a third of my mother's flower garden.

Maya and I kissed and hugged, refusing to let go until the driver cleared his throat. I wanted to beg her to stay, but I couldn't get the words out.

"I have to go," she said, her eyes searching mine one last time. Her hand caressed my cheek.

"I know."

She waited for me to say something profound. Anything at all. But I had been struck dumb. "Good-bye, Garfunkel," she said.

I've thought of a million things I should have said in that moment, but they all came too late and I was left with just my eyes to express what I felt. After she found her seat and the door hissed shut she waved a soft little beauty queen wave from the back of the bus. I stood there alone in the street watching the bus pull away.

When I turned to go back to work, I could see Martha in the window watching me. I looked down the street one more time as the bus tugged the dust into little airborne drifts, chugging up the rise to the east. When I looked back at the lobby window, Martha was still there watching me. Caught spying, she looked away.

I think I understand now why Lefty Schlosser never slapped an artificial limb on his stump. It would have just hung there, maybe fooling folks at a distance. But you could never fool yourself. Sometimes when he dozed off, he said he could feel the arm throbbing, the fist clenching, and somehow that made him feel better about the loss. I always thought it was the whiskey talking, but I know now it wasn't. You lose things as you go through this life. Precious things drop away like shiny coins sneaking through a hole in your pocket. For a long while it hurts, but the ache reminds you that yes, yes indeed, you once had something precious.

PEOPLE WILL
DISAPPOINT YOU

Tanya gave birth to an eleven-pound baby boy on September 11, a full two weeks past her due date. Butch was there through the whole thing, though Sela Rosemount argued at first that it just didn't seem proper for a man to be in the room. She was old school. But Tanya insisted, and Sela, tough as she was, knew when she was licked.

I wondered if that would be the end of it, if the child would drive a wedge between Butch and the whirlwind infatuation with Tanya. It was hard to fathom that he would settle in at her side and never leave. But that's the way it worked.

Tanya named the boy Monte, and that lasted through the baptism, but after that, everyone called the kid Tex. In the beginning, the boy was a dead ringer for Hawkeye Wilson, but over the years, he began to hobble bowlegged like Butch, drawl like him, and even though he never got as big, he got sturdy and barrel-chested and grew a neck thick as a stump.

As I saw Butch and Tanya and Tex over the years and the beautiful family they had become, I thought about the decision Hawkeye had made when he learned of Tanya's pregnancy. Back then, most men did the right thing, which is why you saw so many miserable married couples. Because they had done the right thing.

Hawkeye Wilson did the right thing. The only thing is, he did it with someone else. I think he panicked, faced with the idea of permanence, for better or worse, but after he met another girl in Boonesville and dated her for a month, he married *her*! It never made any sense at all to me. The marriage didn't last, of course.

As I watched Tex waddle behind Butch dressed like him, wearing belts with big buckles and his name stamped into the leather, as I saw the easy smiles flow between Butch and Tanya, I wonder if Hawkeye didn't realize his mistake.

When it became obvious that the child favored Hawkeye Wilson, I expected Woof to execute Hawkeye for the breach of loyalty to Tanya. Woof and I talked about it one night. We'd been shooting hoops at the court by the church, jacking up impossible shots under the shine of the streetlights. The only place to sit was the church steps, so that is where we sat, on the cool concrete, sniffing the sweet scent of freshly cut grass.

It wasn't right, I said, what Hawkeye had done.

Woof sighed. "People are gonna disappoint you, Bones."

What an awful thing to say, I thought at the time. What kind of dictum is that to live by? *People are gonna dis-*

appoint you. Know it. Expect it. I did not like hearing that, because idealists do not want to know the truth. But in time, I came to accept that it was true. I also came to believe that he was not saying it to be harsh—that he had gotten so cold and pragmatic that he had lost all hope in people. He just understood that people were, well, people.

I realized that I had disappointed Woof many times, and he had disappointed me, but at the end of the day we were still going to be friends. Even when we were hundreds, then thousands of miles apart, that never changed. The bond never wavered, because more than loyalty, we afforded each other compassion.

I never stopped being disappointed when people disappointed me. I never started expecting it. But I never allowed myself to be surprised when it happened, either.

ANOTHER RAMBLER

Tiny was pissed. He went blowing out of the city shop, toward the open bay doors of the Farmers Union, three hundred pounds of consternation stomping thunderously up the street. Close behind, scampering three steps to one of Tiny's giant stomps, was Bull Malone, trying to catch up but attempting to appear dignified in a three-piece suit just the same.

"Son of a bitch!" Tiny said. "I don't believe it!"

"Whatsa problem, Tiny?" Irv asked, peering up from the disassembled remains of a John Deere.

"I'll tell you what my problem is," Tiny said. "We got a goddamn comedian for a mayor."

"C'mon, Tiny," Bull panted, finally catching up. "It's tradition."

"Bullshit!" Tiny roared. "You just did it because you are a cruel sumbitch!"

"What'd he do?" I asked.

"He got another Rambler for a police car! That's what he did!"

"Now, Tiny," Bull soothed, with a shit-eating grin as wide as his face, "a Rambler is a fine automobile."

"I hate fuckin' Ramblers! You knew goddamn well I wanted a Plymouth. Hell, I woulda took a Chevy or a Ford, even. But a Rambler! Little old ladies drive Ramblers."

"On the contrary," I said, as Ella rumbled past and rolled through the stop sign in front of us. "Little old ladies drive Corvettes."

"That's exactly my point!" Tiny said. "I think. It's embarrassing pulling someone over in a Rambler. Irv, how would you like to ride to jail in the back of a goddamn Rambler?"

Irv studied the label on his third Nesbitt's of the morning. "I wouldn't like it at all," he decided.

"See! See!" Tiny shouted, hopping up and down, pointing his finger into Bull's grin. "The people have spoken! No one wants to get arrested in a Rambler! It's cruel and unusual punishment is what it is! Bones! Ain't there some sort of statute against that?"

"I think it's in the Constitution," I said. "Or Hammurabi's Code. Or the Magna Carta. One of those."

"See!" Tiny said. "Shit, having Spook blow that car up was about the best day of my life. If we ever find that crazy bastard, we ought to give him a commendation before we hang his ass."

"Tiny, Ramblers have had a glorious history in law enforcement," Bull said.

"Yeah. So did the Pinkertons. You don't see many of them around these days."

"Now, Tiny, we got a deal on the car . . ."

"Of course, you got a deal on the car. Thing is fourteen fucking years old. How long did it take you to find another '63?"

"There *was* considerable effort involved," Bull said. "Me and the missus drove all the way to Valentine, Nebraska, to pick it up."

"Who had it there?" Tiny snapped. "Undertaker?"

"Hairdresser," Bull said.

Irv blew soda through his nose.

I thought Tiny was going to bust a vein right then and there. "You are one malicious son of a bitch," he rasped, before resuming his Godzilla stomp.

Bull sighed and stretched out his stubby arms as if to embrace the world. "Looks like it's going to be a glorious day, huh, fellas?"

BETTER TO BE A NOVELIST

It would be easier, I think, if I were a novelist. Better to be the god of your own little world, sliding characters here and there, tying up their plastic little lives with tidy red ribbons, smiting those deserving, giving the heroes capes and commanding them to leap buildings in a single bound. It would be for the best. I could write happily ever afters. The good guy would always sweep Nell from the path of the onrushing train. Her ample breasts would heave against his chest, and I would fade the chapter then out of decency and modesty.

However, I am stuck with the truth as I am best able to recall it. It would be easier if we were always well prepared, always aware, as we plod toward one event or another. We would have destiny scheduled like a dental appointment, and we would take notes along the way.

Yes, officer, I remember vividly. It was precisely 9:32 P.M. Cat Stevens was on the radio being followed by a moon shadow, moon shadow. Three vehicles were ahead of me, one behind, all proceeding north, when a 1977 green Oldsmobile with a strip of chrome missing on the driver's side door proceeded into the intersection without yielding the right of way. Oh yes, of course, I got the license plate, officer. It was TJB911.

Instead, what you are left with is the echo of a big crash and the explanation that "the stupid bastard came out of nowhere. The color of the car? White, I think. Maybe blue."

See, a novelist doesn't have to bother with all of that. He just makes up details as he goes. If he wants it to be a white car, it sure as hell is going to be a white car. A reporter has it tougher. Through a painstaking process, you have got to figure what happened and how it happened. Then, when the report is dutifully printed, people will pooh-pooh and say you are full of shit because they heard from a friend of a friend who heard a rumor about a guy who was actually there, and that's not the way it was at all.

A novelist is pretty much understood to be full of shit. There is no deception. Or rather, deception is the objective. I'm gonna write me a novel someday and just below the title where the publishers always print boldly **A NOVEL**, as if this is some sort of profound new thing, I will insist that they print **FULL OF SHIT.**

It would be better to be a novelist.

Then things could work out just so.

You would get to be God.

Then the ones you love wouldn't get hurt.

Maybe once, in all the times he had gone fishing, had Joe Big Cloud forgotten the worms. He had almost reached the river's edge when he realized it, so he walked back toward the courthouse.

At the Farmers Union Oil station, I was already hustling. Anxious farmers picked up fuel and cotter keys and other odds and ends, nervous that an early snow might roll in before the corn was safely in the crib. At 6:50 A.M., I backed the bulk truck out, clearing the mechanics bay for the day's problems.

Meanwhile, Ella Peterson was running terribly late. That chipped tooth was giving her all sorts of grief, and she'd had to beg the dentist to open early. She had to be there at precisely 7:30 A.M. I heard the engine of her Corvette winding as Ella roared away from her driveway, tires spitting gravel, screeching when they gripped pavement. There wasn't much traffic.

I stopped to admire the lines of the car heading toward me as I always did. Out of the corner of my eye, I spotted something flickering down the incline of the street to the east, toward the intersection. At first, I could not make out what it was as it darted in brief flickers past the trees obscuring my vision. When it reached the intersection a split second before the Corvette, I could see what it was. Coop was grinning back at Charlie Brown as the dog scrambled to catch up to the accelerating skateboard.

I do not remember the sound. There must have been

a sickening thud as the chrome bumper flipped him into the windshield and over the car. Tires must have squealed as Ella braked much too late.

I must have screamed. I must have. But I cannot remember. The first thing I heard—as if the volume switch had suddenly been switched back on—was a wail from inside the car.

I ran in what seemed like slow motion toward the back of the car, so afraid of what I would see.

Coop was sprawled on his back.

Unconscious.

Twitching.

Twitching.

His legs were folded at the shins and blood flowed from his ear. And he was twitching. Charlie Brown, whose back had been broken, dragged his useless hind legs to Coop, whimpering.

I heard the crunch of gravel as Joe came out of nowhere and ran toward Coop in slow motion like me. I must have yelled for him to do something, my shouts joining Ella's wailing. But I don't remember. I remember the awful hopelessness. I do not remember screaming.

Joe extended his arms to the pink morning sky as he kneeled at Coop's side.

He held them high for the longest time.

A gurgle came from Coop's chest and then he stopped breathing.

Jesus. Oh, Jesus.

Joe looked scared. And that scared me, if it was possible I could be any more frightened. Then, slowly, far too slowly, Joe closed his eyes, breathed a deep breath, exhaled, and lowered his hands.

They hovered indecisively over the body.

ANOTHER FUNERAL

It rained the day of the funeral.

Most of the leaves had fallen from the branches, so there was no shelter from the persistent, pelting drops. No one had thought to bring an umbrella, though the clouds were evident from the first light of the day.

It was a small funeral.

Astor Malone said a few words over the grave. The sound of the rain on the fallen golden maple leaves filled the gaps between the words. Astor smiled softly when he was done.

There was a brief silence.

"He was a good dog," Coop said from his wheelchair, his sodden hair plastered against his forehead. Joe and Ella, Mom and Dad, and I all agreed that Charlie Brown had indeed been a good dog. The finest kind.

"Maybe we can get you a puppy, Coop," Mom offered.

Coop fingered the casts on his legs, thumping one of them with his knuckle, listening to the hollow sound. "Maybe.

But, I think maybe I just need to miss Charlie Brown for a while, first."

"Whatever you want, honey."

We buried Charlie Brown under the crooked old maple tree near the alley where he had snoozed on hot days. We had called it Charlie's Tree, even then. After that, it was a monument. Mom and Coop planted a small ring of flowers around the thick trunk the next spring.

Ella hugged Coop and wept after the funeral, her crippled back perfectly hunched for the task. Coop held her tight as she cried. "Everything is going to be all right," he said as he hugged her. He hugged her hard. She yelped at the sharp jolt of pain.

"My back feels like fire," she said. "I think I need to go home and lie down."

Joe stayed by the small plot and said a few words of prayer to honor Charlie Brown. Everyone else moved inside for coffee and cake, but I watched from the foot of the steps.

It stopped raining. With the faint clatter of coffee cups on saucers inside, I waited as Joe walked to me. "You want some cake and coffee? Mom's serving inside."

"No. No, thanks," Joe said, breathing deeply. "I think I'll stay outside and enjoy the smell of the rain." He motioned toward the house and lowered his voice. "How is Coop doing?"

"Well, the doctor says he's never seen bones mend so fast. He says Coop ought to be walking in a few weeks. His legs won't be the same, but the doctor says that after the way they were splintered, it's a miracle."

Joe got a faraway look.

"So Joe," I ventured. "You brought Coop back. I thought you didn't heal people."

"I didn't know if I could. I'd be lying if I said my faith didn't waver when I saw Coop like that. But I heard a voice that gave me strength."

"Whose voice?" Astor Malone interrupted, opening the screen door of the porch and stepping out with coffee in hand. "Did you hear the voice of God?" He was only half-kidding.

Silence.

"It was my mother," Joe said. He turned to look at me. His lips quivered. When he had composed himself he continued. "She spoke to me like she did when I was a boy. 'Be brave,' she said. She told me to have faith."

I think there was a tear in his eye.

It could have been a raindrop.

I can't say for sure.

A SMALL PRICE TO PAY
FOR A MIRACLE

It was not unusual in the high plains for boys to do the work
of men. Families of fifteen or sixteen children were not uncommon in the early days when the settlers turned the prairie upside down. Farms and ranches are work, and work
requires workers. It had not changed much in my day.

Second grade boys, and lots of girls, too, would drive
their fathers' grain trucks from the field at harvesttime.
Drivers passing through on the back roads were startled to
see ghosts or the decapitated driving clanking, smoking
pickup trucks with fenders dented by malcontent cattle. But
when the visitors got closer, they would witness tiny, cal-
lused hands on the wheel and small eyes peering through it.

But children grow up. Eventually, the eyes rise above
the wheel, and the three-inch cheater blocks of wood are
unclamped from the clutch, brake, and accelerator.

But if the cows don't kill you, if you don't smother in
a grain bin of spring wheat, if you don't fall off the back of

the tractor and under the slicing blades of the disc, if you don't leap from the hay mound with a rope around your neck after the banker shuts you down—if you survive all that, you will dry up anyway.

The prairie and buttes and their sun and wind, which have kissed you and nurtured you and loved you, will shrink you and humble you, leaving you hunched and bent, once again peering through the steering wheel as you drive.

It is not supposed to be reversible.

The doctor was astonished. The ravages of arthritis and osteoporosis had almost completely vanished. For the first time in decades, there were complaints from the parishioners seated directly behind Ella Peterson. The billowing Sunday hats that would have embarrassed Carmen Miranda had always been situated low enough and the pulpit high enough that obstructionism in the House of the Lord was not an issue.

Astor intervened when Ella's back grew straight and tall again and negotiated a treaty involving, if not disarmament, then at least smaller hats.

It was a small price to pay for a miracle.

Around town, we considered it the way most of us do when we happen upon a miracle. We view it as an aberration. We don't really want to acknowledge what we feel. We lean back as the waitress pours another cup of coffee and then resume our discussion of the healing. "Isn't that something," we say, but not much more. People might start to think you're crazy if you started to believe in miracles and such. Better to keep them bound tightly within the confines of the New Testament.

But Ella couldn't stop talking about it. After she had thought about it, she came to the conclusion that somehow Joe had shared his power with a gimp-legged retarded boy. Public reaction was typical. That Ella was just an old eccentric with impressive posture and a hot car was the consensus. But despite all the public pooh-poohing of the notion that God's hand might be at work, one or two geriatrics dropped in to see Coop.

I was just in the neighborhood, mind you, and I brought a fresh pumpkin pie. You do like pumpkin, don't you, Coop? And anyway, I was wondering . . . and I know it sounds silly, but the pain gets so bad sometimes that . . .

Hanky Bendewald's palsy went away. Cootie Sperling started to hear better. Which meant her husband had to break a forty-year habit of muttering about her.

Word of the healings spread like a ripple in a pond past the confines of Pale Butte, and as the months passed, the desperate arrived, lining up in the porch of my parents' house. It started to get scary and overwhelming for Mom and Dad, so Astor stepped in, and all requests were henceforth steered through him. It was just as well that Coop found another vocation. His legs couldn't take the grind of mowing anymore.

Eventually, even with appointments and structure,

the flow of visitors became too much for a family home, so, with the permission of the church council, Astor moved the organ from the loft and built Coop an office of his very own.

COMPLICATIONS

That's how it all should have ended, and it seemed for a while that everything would settle pretty much back to normal. It was a quiet fall and the farmers had a good crop. The elevator had to pile grain on the ground because the bins were full and the boxcars running late. The birds grew fat. But winter came early that year and it came with complications.

I was walking into the drugstore for another package of black licorice Smith Brothers cough drops and a box of tissues when I met Grumpy Mindeman walking out. He was wearing familiar-looking rose-colored sunglasses.

"Sorry, Bones, I didn't mean to startle you."

I studied the shades. I felt a little queasy. "You just buy those?"

"Nope. Snagged 'em ice fishing yesterday, out south of town. Pulled 'em right out of the muck. They cleaned up good, didn't they?"

"Nice," I said, wiping my oozing nostrils with my mitten.

"I kind of like the way the world looks through them," he said. "Sort of makes everything peaceful-like."

"Catch anything else?"

"Dozen perch. Fattest ones I ever saw in winter. They've been eating good."

"Uh, huh."

"Want some? They fry up great this time of year."

"Nah. But thanks."

The next day he went on a four-day drunk and lost the shades. When he finally returned to his hot spot to drill another hole, the fishing was not good. In fact, he kept snagging something under the ice. He lost two hooks, so when he felt the third snag he pulled hard.

It could have been a stick, he thought as he reeled it through the circle of open water. Maybe a chunk of driftwood. When it floated closer he could see it was flesh. Probably a hunk of rotting carp. It was about three inches long and resembled a ragged white chunk of sodden sausage. As he removed the hook, he began retching. It had a fingernail.

In three hours, a dive team from the county was hacking away at the ice with Tiny supervising. It took a big hole to extricate the body, which was bloated up to twice the size of a normal man and chewed up by the fish. At first, one diver tugged hard on an arm in an effort to bring the body to the surface. The skin sloughed off the bone, a white lump of limp, rotting meat, which was secured in a body bag by puking volunteers onshore. The problem, the divers discovered, was the body was weighted down by a gunnysack full of rocks tied to the legs by a length of pale green rope. Tiny secured the rope, the rocks, and the gunnysack as evidence.

It did not take the county coroner long to rule the cause of death, and it wasn't drowning. The dead man, still wearing plaid and paisley polyester, which stretched beautifully to accommodate the bloat, had died from blunt force trauma. The time of death? About mid-August, the coroner figured. You wouldn't get that kind of rot and bloat in December's icy water. The dead man's bones were splinters.

The investigators concluded that there was only one cowboy who used a green lariat. Then more than one helpful citizen remembered Butch's splinted fingers and the bruise on Woof's cheek at the funeral of Rose Iris Schwartz. Who had a bigger motive?

Butch and Woof were arrested, but neither one of them confessed. Even when they were each offered a reduced sentence to testify against the other, they remained silent. Butch insisted his lariat had been stolen the night of the fire right out the back of his pickup parked in Sela Rosemount's driveway. He hadn't missed it for a few days and then didn't report it because with all of the other hubbub, it didn't seem like a big deal. That was his story.

The whole thing hit the papers with a vengeance, and some nosy Boonesville reporter played it up like the death of Spook was some great loss to the community. All the attention gave State's Attorney Josh Rustan ample opportunity to preen for the cameras. Of course, all the fuss meant he would have to make good, and folks around here couldn't begin to remember his last conviction.

The case against Woof was iffy, but that hunk of green lariat figured to be enough to nail Butch. It looked like Josh Rustan was about to break his losing streak.

Tanya Schwartz stopped eating. Soon she couldn't nurse the baby anymore, and Sela Rosemount put the child on formula. They limited visitors at the jail, but the fact that Tanya could visit her brother and her fiancé in one trip did make it convenient. At least there was that.

The judge appointed separate lawyers for Woof and Butch and each encouraged his client to roll over on his friend because lawyers are schooled to be disloyal fucks. "Somebody should be there for Tanya," they argued. "One of you." After nine days of interrogation, it was a powerful argument. But Woof continued to maintain that he wasn't really sure who this Spook guy was. Never heard of him. And Butch insisted he didn't like Woof enough to invite him to a homicide—even if he ever had planned to do such a thing.

Butch's attorney got the idea to have him marry Tanya real quick-like, so as his spouse, she couldn't be forced to testify against him. The cops figured she knew *something*. Besides, he argued, the jury might not want to convict a dirt-poor rancher with a young bride and a baby. This got Josh Rustan all riled up. The media king could smell a conviction, and be damned if he'd have it ruined at this stage of the game. But those damned defense attorneys have a way of complicating things.

Then it got worse. It seems Tiny had misplaced the evidence. Not all of it, mind you. The gunnysack was still there. And the rocks. But be damned if he could find that pale green lariat.

"Well, well," Butch's attorney argued. "Maybe we ought to just plea-bargain this thing out. You know, save the tax-payers the expense of a long trial." Sure, Butch's was the only green lariat around. But who's to say it wasn't just a length of rope turned green by algae? It was just too damn bad it was missing. And the gunnysack? "Hell, you might as well indict half the farmers in the county who plant DEKALB seed," the lawyer argued.

So Josh Rustan was not exactly brimming with confidence the day Joe Big Cloud walked in and confessed to the murder of Ernest Collins Jr. Joe couldn't remember the particulars exactly. It all happened so fast, you know. But he had done it, all right. He insisted.

Joe knew exactly when and where the crime had been committed—at the grave of Spook's mother on the night of August 16, 1977. Sure enough, after the snow had been swept away, the evidence of a scuffle remained. There were gouges in the dirt from desperate heels and a spackling of dried blood on the monument. And that explained the small grains of red granite under Spook's fingernails. He had been clinging to the unpolished edges of his mother's tombstone before he died.

Only the murderer could have known so many details, Josh Rustan said. Case closed. Butch and Woof tried briefly to argue the point, but Tanya and two defense attorneys managed to shush them real quick. Besides, who you gonna believe? Two west river punks who have spent the last two weeks denying the most obvious facts, or a holy man like Joe Big Cloud?

Josh Rustan was all too glad to get a signed confession. He paraded it for the cameras like a teenage boy after a successful panty raid.

TOUCH WISELY

There was a long line of visitors to see the guilty man the day before he was shipped to a county cell to await sentencing. Coop had managed to talk his way in twice. I followed Bull and Astor Malone.

Joe was calm, and me, I was trying.

"Geez, Joe, Butch and Woof would have gotten off, anyway," I said. "Josh Rustan had nothing on them, and anyway, when was the last time he won a case?"

Joe peered through the bars to the right and the left to make sure no one else could hear. "I wasn't willing to take that chance. One life for two is a good trade."

"But Joe. You could have at least *waited* to see how the trial went. If things weren't going good, well, that's when a guy could jump in and confess! It would be all sorts of dramatic. That's the way it should have happened."

Joe nodded knowingly. Then he paused for a beat.

"My timing was right. My work here is done."

"How can you say that," I snapped, then quickly regretted my insolence. I was not so angry as I was desperate. I had lost Maya, my poet, and was still haunted by the vision of her face disappearing behind swirls of brown dust, and now I would lose my teacher and friend. And I felt like the loneliest man on earth.

"Joe," I said, "you opened my eyes to a world I could not see before. Now I am beginning to see my path. I've learned a lot from you and . . ."

Joe waited awhile for the end of my sentence. When he was convinced it would remain forever incomplete, he spoke.

"It is good our paths joined. But now I must walk my path and you must walk yours. You do not need anyone to show you the way. All the answers are within you. If you stop and listen, you will hear your heart tell you the answers. Stop for a moment and try to feel the river of life. Find the flow."

"Jesus, Joe . . ."

"You have touched me, my friend. Each day, we touch others. It can be positive. It can be negative. It can be neutral. Now imagine, Bones, if we remain conscious of the touch so that when we meet a stranger, we treat them with kindness, and they, in turn, will be inclined to treat others with compassion. We are nothing without the touch of others. It is a simple thing, and it is a powerful thing. It is a sacred thing. Touch wisely."

Before I left, he stretched his hand through the bars to rest on my shoulder. "Bones, will you do one thing for me?"

"Of course."

"Bull Malone will need to hire a new man. And he'll need a place to stay. Would you see that my things are removed?"

That is when I wept.

The room was cold and quiet. Joe had packed everything neatly and had tagged the boxes and his sparse collection of furniture as well.

He gave Butch the chrome table, which sat forevermore in the ranch kitchen. Over the years, I shared many meals at that table. I watched Tex grow taller and heard his voice deepen. Oh, the stories I told him! Stories about his Uncle Woof—the rascal! Stories about Joe Big Cloud—true stories—stories hardly embellished at all.

Regretfully, I would drive away alone from that bold little ranch, and as I accelerated, leaving Butch, Tanya, and Tex behind me like memories, I would notice the ache in my face. It was from smiling.

Woof got the chessboard. He held his head in his hands the day I gave it to him, and he looked so small as he sat there. Even when he looked up, he would not look at me.

There was a small worn wooden jewelry box with Maya's name lettered neatly on a tag. Inside was a near-perfect crystal the size of a nickel. I mailed it to Stanford.

Coop got Joe's medicine bundle. I half-expected the contents to glow and spark with magic, but there was not much to see—a piece of turtle shell, the tip of a buffalo horn, a shark's tooth, a silver dollar so worn the date could not be read, cloth bundles of various foul-smelling herbs and powders tied with butcher's string and a meadowlark feather. Coop added two items to the menagerie—a Hot Wheels version of a powder blue Corvette and a few clumps of Charlie Brown's fur, plucked from the old rug in the back porch where Charlie used to sleep.

I got Joe's old Dynaco tube amp speakers, and the records. Funny thing. As good as that amp and those speakers were, for the longest time, when I played Joe's albums, they didn't sound right—they all had a melancholy lilt. Everything was a dirge.

There was a brown paper package with my name on it as well, and inside . . . My God, it was beautiful! It was a buckskin shirt expertly tanned to a creamy white. Only at the seams and at the edges where the leather had grown stiff did it hint at its age.

The Ghost Shirt was intricately painted with turtles, meadowlarks, stars, and crescent moons in reds and yellows, blues and white. Long, gentle tassels draped from the waist. They danced in these shirts until the visions came, before the dance was banned. Some said you could wear such a shirt and become invisible. Long ago, the Lakota wore the Ghost Shirts with the promise that no white man's bullet could penetrate.

I have never been shot, so I would have to say that it works.

It did not dawn on me for quite some time what the Ghost Shirt meant. It was more than a gift from a friend. I remembered Joe's lament that he had no son to whom he could pass the secrets of the Ghost Dance, and I understood eventually that I had become that son, and Coop had become the healer and Joe's son as well. I think he saw us all as his children—Maya, Woof, and Butch, too—and that solved the mystery of his sacrifice. Joe did what any father would do.

I did what any son would do. On Joe's last night in Pale Butte, I kept vigil outside the door of the jail with Bertram Sumpter, and I wore the Ghost Shirt because it made me feel powerful and closer to Joe. I begged Tiny to let me spend the night inside with Joe, but he wouldn't.

" 'Gainst regulations."

"When did you ever follow regulations?"

He was still trying to come up with the answer when I stomped out. So I sat with Bertram and his 12-gauge shotgun in the chilly night, and Tiny spent the night at his desk.

I brought along a fifth of Old Coon Hound whiskey—Bertram's poison—and you know what? When he's loaded, Bertram Sumpter is a pretty good guy.

MAYBE HOUDINI
COULD HAVE DONE IT

The state sent a van with a driver and a guard to transfer the prisoner at seven the next morning. When they arrived, they had to jostle Tiny awake at his desk. Out front, Bertram was pretty lively, all things considered. Sleepily, like a confused bear at the end of hibernation, Tiny rooted deep into his pocket for the keys and led the men back to take Joe Big Cloud away.

Then all hell broke loose.

The cell was empty. And the door was still locked.

Now maybe Harry Houdini could have shook that can. Maybe someone like that. There were no windows. And even if he had gotten the cell door open, there were two more locked steel doors to open before you could get to the front entrance where Bertram Sumpter had sat all night with an over-and-under 12-gauge.

Lotsa folks thought it must have been one of Tiny's convenient oversights. But Bertram swore up and down no mortal man had passed through those doors.

Still, Tiny got suspended, and the state pushed to have him fired. But Bull Malone stood firm and would not do it. Tiny was the unfortunate victim of circumstance, he said. "Ain't no law against a man havin' a string of bad luck."

They set up roadblocks and rousted bums in rail yards in three states, but the bloodhounds never got a whiff. They took them to Joe's apartment to get a scent, and the dogs all wagged their tails happily like they were greeting an old friend.

Everyone had a theory about what had happened to Joe.

"Spontaneous combustion," said Grumpy.

"Secret tunnel," guessed Sally Prunty.

"Alien abduction," said Sarah Leesburg.

But I liked Coop's version best. "Angels saved him. It was the angels!"

We were walking one day, Coop and I, and we discovered a sparrow outside a picture window in someone's front yard. You lose a lot of birds that way. They see the window, and they think they can fly right through it. Maybe a Houdini bird could do it. But the rest end up as worm food. And I suppose the worms figure it's only fair.

Coop picked up the body, stroking its feathers back into place. The bird had not yet begun to rot. I was about to tell Coop to set the bird down when it cocked its head and preened right there in his hand. When the bird regained its bearings, it flapped its wings and fluttered off. It turned a graceful circle over our heads.

Then it smacked right back into the picture window.

I know the evidence is circumstantial. One of those Harvard scientists would say that. The Lazarus bird might have just been stunned when Coop picked it up. Maybe he wasn't dead at all. Believe what you will.

After the bird hit the window a second time, Coop looked at me.

"Leave him there," I said. "He had his chance."

This healing thing with Coop got pretty big. Once he was mentioned in the same *Time* magazine article as Oral Roberts. That was about the time Oral started seeing nine-hundred-foot Jesuses. They quoted Coop as saying he had seen a thousand-foot Jesus—a *"my God's bigger than your God" sort of thing*—but Coop always maintained he had said no such thing.

We were sitting one Saturday morning at his office, watching Popeye cartoons, wondering just why Bluto had become Brutus, when I finally got around to asking him about the big Jesus. Coop got the same sheepish look that always appeared on his face when he had fibbed, but he insisted he had been misquoted.

"That's good enough for me," I said, rising to leave.

I turned before I reached the door. "Can I come over again next Saturday?"

"You bet," he said, his eyes only briefly leaving the screen. "I get lonely sometimes."

"Gee, Coop, you have a dozen people come to see you every day."

"Yeah," he said. He stared at his hands for a moment. "But they only want me to fix their broken parts. They don't want to spend time with me. And some of them are scared of me. Now I know how Spook felt."

I didn't know what to say to that.

"Coop, is there anything I can bring you next time?"

Gum, he said. He was running out of gum.

He looked away from the television when my hand reached the latch.

"Jesus loves you," he said.

"Good."

Coop did not get a salary as such, but the church did receive an almost alarming number of donations from a constant stream of lepers. Astor insisted there would be no payment required. That might cause Coop to lose the gift, he reasoned. But money poured in anyway.

The facades of the Main Street businesses were refurbished as every business thrived with the visitations. Crucifixes sold out as fast as Sally Prunty got them in. They sold locks of Coop's hair at the barbershop until Astor made them stop. The bar started selling T-shirts that read, *I got healed at the Mecca Bar.*

The city coffers bulged from the city sales tax, and Mayor Bull Malone relented, finally, and ordered Tiny a brand-new Plymouth police cruiser with a protective cage for the backseat. Irv was the first to ride in it after his arrest for writing his name in urine in the snow on Main Street.

Just for the record, he didn't like it.

That was the night of Hawkeye Wilson's second wedding. Woof was best man. It was the last big shindig held at St. Andrew's. Visitors seeking healing swelled the congregation on Sundays until they began to squeeze the regulars out. So a new St. Andrew's was built, a majestic, modern, tan brick building with glorious stained glass. The old church was converted into a chapel, and Coop maintained his office in the loft. They added a daybed with a small kitchen, and slowly Coop was weaned from the family home.

There was quite a debate between Fred Sturm and the deacons when it came to naming the chapel, but the impasse was broken by Coop.

So the Chapel of Saint Joseph it was.

REFLECTIONS IN THE RIVER

Maya came back to Pale Butte two more times. The first was when her Grandpa Gus died, and she flew back for the funeral with her boyfriend. It almost killed me. The second time she came back to bury her grandmother. This time she arrived with two children—a boy and a girl—each with a pug nose spackled with freckles—and the boyfriend who had become a husband. And I went numb.

"This is your Uncle Bones," she told the youngsters, from her haunches, looking them in the eye, as her husband looked on. A crystal necklace dangled from her neck.

It would have been easy for her husband to resent me. The truth is, I tried to resent him. But he just nodded when I asked if I might take his wife for a drive so we could talk. You have to be real secure in your relationship to allow that.

"I've heard a lot about you," he said, grasping my hand with a firm grip.

"Yeah, well, I hope you didn't believe it," I said.

He chuckled.

Conversation always seemed to come easier for me on the back roads. Woof and I covered a million miles as we stared ahead, only occasionally glancing out of the corners of our eyes as we spoke. Of course, Woof hadn't been home for years. He'd disappeared into the radio. A weekend job on the air in Boonesville took him to Denver and KIMN and then to WLS in Chicago, where he replaced John Records Landecker. He got fired after a while—for not being Landecker, I guess.

He bounced around so much sometimes my letters would come back ADDRESS UNKNOWN. And sometimes even Tanya wouldn't know for a few months where he had gone. Some nights I drove the gravel alone, tuning in the AM stations. Voices would drift in and drift away again, and one night I heard my friend's voice on KOMA out of Oklahoma City. He rode the wave of the intro to the Spencer Davis Group like a surfer. *Gimme Some Lovin'*. Hey! After fifteen minutes or so, the signal began melting away and Woof went with it. In the business, they say he was one of the great ones.

Maya and I tried to find Butch that day, but he and Tanya were at a Little League game in Boonesville. Tex, with his amazing curveball, was pitching in the nightcap. So it was just the two of us, a six-pack of Grain Belt, and WLS crackling through on the radio.

"Bones?"

"Yeah?"

"Whatever possessed you to buy this Edsel?"

I sipped, steering the gargantuan wheel with two fingers. I hadn't really given it much thought. The Larsons had listed it on the auction along with the tractors, machinery, and a lifetime worth of dreams lost to hail, drought, and bad times. And when it came up for auction, and the bidding stalled at $900, I jumped in. I got it for $935.

"I guess maybe this old car and me were going to be linked forever in the stories they tell in the coffee shop anyway," I said. "No sense in running from it."

"No sense in embracing it, either, is there?"

"I'm good with who I am. It's your fault, really. You're the one who gave me the confidence to be me."

"I did that?"

"Uh, huh."

"If this is what it has led to, I am truly sorry."

"It's okay. Really."

We sat and sipped like nothing had changed.

"You're happy?" I asked, fearing the answer.

"Very," she said. And it hurt. "Thank you," she added.

"What did I do?"

"You were wise enough to let me go. I would have stayed here with you."

It was hard to hear her say that, and she realized it as soon as the words were out. We stared ahead at the road creeping beneath us "But, in some ways, I'm glad I left when I did. It would have been hard to see Woof and Butch in jail and . . . and Joe. I was so disappointed in Joe. I never believed he could hurt anyone."

My throat got thick. "But Spook killed Rose. He wasn't going to stop. If there was ever a righteous killing, this was it."

"Yes. Yes, I know. But, I had Joe up here . . ." She held her hand high toward heaven and slowly lowered it. "And, now he's down here. With us. Human."

I felt nauseous. It wasn't right that Joe's memory should be sullied like this. It wasn't fair. Isn't it something that we will defend a memory just like we defend home and country?

"Joe didn't do it," I blurted.

"You mean it *was* Woof and Butch. . . . Oh, Christ. . . ."

"No. No!" I stopped the car abruptly, throwing her forward. She braced her hand on the dashboard. She stared at me, but I could not face her, so I spoke to the windshield and the beam of light spread before it.

"You see . . . after Rose died . . ."

"Oh, Bones . . ."

"There comes a time to cull the herd. . . . Don't you see? He wasn't going to stop."

"Not you, Bones. . . . Please, tell me it wasn't you."

But I couldn't. If you want to get right down to it, it was Nellie Fox who did it.

I don't know how long we sat staring at the beam of light in silence, but a chill settled between us that never completely left. I had salvaged Joe's standing in her eyes at the expense of my own.

"I should get back," Maya said, and her voice sounded thin. "I should put the kids to bed. I hate missing bedtime."

She smiled wanly. "Remember that day on the bench when you told me how I was going to be all domestic, scrubbing floors and such?" She laughed softly, and though it was a little forced, I remembered how much I missed hearing that sound. "Well, you were right," she said. "And it's wonderful. I've decided that being a parent is a pretty high calling."

She kissed me on the cheek when I dropped her off and then, with the door ajar, she leaned back in as if she had forgotten something and kissed me tenderly on the lips, but her lips were cool.

After that, it was mostly Christmas cards with pictures of red-haired kids growing up too fast. That and the certain knowledge that somewhere inside she still loved me, and I loved her, and it doesn't matter that we did.

For me, the journey led many places. But the path led home in the end. That was the thing that surprised me. And I think that is the thing Joe always knew would happen. Nowadays, I drop a line into the river when the weather co-operates. I always sit where Joe did. I tried fishing a couple of other spots, but it just didn't feel right. Once in a while, a child will plop down beside me, so I can tell about the good old days just like I said I wouldn't.

A line in the water is an invitation. It calls to passersby. It lures them close.

"Catchin' anything?" they ask. Those are the best days, because in those innocent eyes and faces, I see hope for this old world.

I was reeling my line in one day after two hours of

sitting with a young towheaded chap who reminded me a lot of the Woof of my childhood. When I pulled in the line, he saw that all I had attached was a sinker.

"Hey, mister, you can't catch fish without a hook."

"Ah, but I was not fishing for fish," I said.

I started to make it a point to fish more regularly, hoping I would see the boy. And I did. I told him all the stories about the old days in Pale Butte and Joe Big Cloud. The boy was a good listener.

"Why do you dance up on the hill sometimes?" he asked one day. "My daddy says you're not quite right in the head," he added without a hint of malice.

"Well, I would prefer being called eccentric. I think maybe we're all eccentric. Some of us act odd behind closed doors. Others don't much care what anyone else thinks. As for the dance? Yes, I dance the Ghost Dance. It's like a prayer. I'm praying for a better world."

"That don't seem so crazy."

"Thanks," I said, tousling his mop. "Maybe one day I'll teach you how to do the dance."

I built a house into the side of the hill below the cemetery where the lambs used to frolic, across from Joe's boulder. Funny, isn't it, that I was so bound and determined to get out of this place, and look where I am now. But after Maya and Woof and Joe left, though, I drifted away, too.

For a while.

I put my memories down on paper—so I could convince myself when I got older that all of this really happened.

Eventually, my work as a stringer for the *Pale Butte Sentinel* landed me a job with the newspaper in Boonesville. I started covering the police beat, which consisted mostly of lost dogs and parking infractions. But the editor said I had an eye for detail, and they let me write a few features. He said he was sorry to see me go when I rode the ferry up the inland passage to Alaska to work as a reporter for the *Juneau Empire*. I got an apartment on Douglas Island, so from my kitchen I could see the cruise ship lights sparkling at night below three-thousand-foot mountains that looked taller because they reached right down to dip their toes in the icy Gastineau Channel.

Wherever I went, I found myself living beside the water.

In Myrtle Beach, I got a condo on the beach, which lasted less than two months before Hurricane Hugo swooped in and scattered Ella Fitzgerald and Peggy Lee and Rosemary Clooney to the wind. After that, I sort of resented South Carolina.

So I moved back to the Dakotas. Mom and Dad were getting older, and I wanted to be closer to them. But more than that, I needed to be on the prairie. I am a child of the plains, and even when I walked beaches barefoot in the supple southern warmth, the buttes called to me like a mother calls a child from the porch steps. So I bounced around from Williston to Sturgis to Belle Fourche and Fargo.

I never made much money working for someone else, so I tried a few things on the side. Dad and I lost almost everything one year when he convinced me to invest in oats. He was an elevator man, I reasoned. He ought to know the grain market.

Hawkeye Wilson laughed when I told him what I had done. That was the weekend of his third wedding. I'd come back to be a groomsman, though he promoted me to best man for his fourth wedding a few years later.

Hawkeye convinced me to trust him and his small brokerage firm in Boonesville with what I had left. When I found out he'd steered me into a Seattle-based company that wrote computer programs, I could have killed him. Dad had been harping about soybeans, and this time I was sure he was right, and I told Hawkeye that was the way to go for sure. I got mad again when he diversified me into a pharmaceutical company that made blood pressure medicine.

He called me on my thirty-ninth birthday.

"Congratulations," he said.

"Big deal. Just another birthday."

"It's your birthday?"

Turns out, my portfolio had hit a million, which for those days meant you had officially made it big. Funny, I always had this theory that God wasn't going to let me get rich until He was sure I wouldn't turn into a giant asshole. But if you look around, you can see that theory doesn't hold water.

The problem with money is that when you get too much of it, it's easy for you to think you're smarter than you are. I was still smart enough to let Hawkeye do the exact opposite of what my father suggested, but I had a stretch where I got fired three times in a row because I started to think I was smarter than my bosses. I was generally right about that, but it didn't excuse the bad attitude. Eventually, I came to the conclusion that I wasn't much good at having people tell me what to do. I liked figuring things out for myself.

I bought the *Pale Butte Sentinel* after Gunnar Smithers died, and surprisingly, made a few bucks. After my portfolio swelled, it didn't seem important that the paper was profitable, but I tried to keep it in the black just as a matter of principle. I sort of felt an obligation. Because if the paper wasn't holding its own when I died or got too tired, it would die, too.

I ran several hundred front-page photographs of yawning, dying fish and several hundred more of yawning, freshly birthed babies. Mutt and I got into a big scrape after he became mayor. He was really pushing for a water project that would bring a pipeline and better water from the Missouri. I skewered him on the editorial page pretty good, complaining about the rate hikes and the tax increases that followed. But when the old city well went dry three years after the pipeline was finished, I started to come around to his point of view.

I sold the company a few years ago to a nice young couple from Colorado, and they treated Mutt a whole lot better. They modernized the whole operation, and naturally, I was against that, too. I was given the title of publisher emeritus, which means I don't have to do anything, but they still let me run a column filled with my formulas for a better world. From the looks of things, no one actually reads it though.

I rode out four stock market crashes. Hawkeye steered me through.

And faith. Faith steered me through.

I started to see that all the insulation you try to wrap around yourself to protect you from the world is a feeble shield. Now, because everything is as clear to me as the Dakota sky, I hardly worry at all. At every turn, when I needed rescuing, I was rescued. I was so busy watching the angels on Woof's shoulders it took some time to notice mine.

Most days, I sit on the patio overlooking the Sneaky River, sipping black market Ethiopian Yergacheffe. I can still see the vehicles go by, but they are silent. My, how I miss the rumble of big gas V-8 motors. I sip my coffee and read everything in the *Boonesville Gazette* except for the stock market stuff. I decided long ago that numbers are really an illusion, and we ought not let them make us feel too good or too bad. I read, and I watch the river flow silently below.

Sometimes it feels like I am watching my life flow past.

There is a river in North Dakota that flows to the north. I know because I stood at the edge of the Red River in Grand Forks a few years back just to see for myself. I snapped small sticks I found along the shore and sprinkled them in the water, and sure enough, slowly, they began to work their way north toward Manitoba.

I remembered that first day with Joe at the river's edge. I have never been able to see a river—the mighty Mississippi or the muddy Missouri—without contemplating the flow of time and life. I see a river and am reminded that there is a plan for me. And for us all.

I will tell you that I have done what Joe said. I have held the ones I love in my heart. I take out the memories and examine them the way wizened old jewelers study diamonds. I look past the occlusions, and I am able to appreciate the brilliance of the reflected light. But sometimes, I want to recapture the idyllic moments. I don't want to just gaze at the light. I want to immerse myself in it like a Baptist baptism.

Shall we gather at the river?

Yes! Yes, we shall.

Sometimes I grow dissatisfied with just keeping them in my heart.

So, I wondered, as I stood there, watching the flow of the river backward to the north, I wondered if I stood here at this spot and wished and prayed and meditated and hoped enough, the backward-flowing water might not serve as a time machine and take me back, so I might touch the moments one more time.

I stood there for a very long time, but all I got was tired.

EPILOGUE

I was driving west on a road I had never driven, twisting dizzily around the mountains, gripping the wheel, gasping at the bottomless valleys. High in the mountains, nestled between the peaks, I drove around a bend at twilight, and that is when I spotted the tidy ranch house I had seen in my dream all those years ago.

The steering wheel spun seemingly of its own volition into the driveway. I heard the pop of a stone flung into the air by the edge of the tire. A light was on inside.

I waited in the car, hoping whoever was inside would walk to the porch and show himself. When that did not happen, I walked to the porch, and I was grateful when it did not creak under my feet.

I stood at the door, just looking at it. Just looking, inspecting the freshly painted wood. I raised my fist to knock, but I could not bring myself to disrupt the solitude. I stepped off the porch and walked around to the window.

I looked up at the sky to marvel at the purple sunset,

and I waited for the rush of a divine wind. I waited for the sun to come streaking backward across the sky. But it did not. Night animals rustled and chirped softly in the grass.

Then I looked in the small window. A beautiful, tiny, gray-haired woman sat in profile at a humble kitchen table. She had the most lovely, warm smile. But she was not smiling at me. At the end of the table, older now—much older now—was my friend Joe Big Cloud. His hair was gray, too, the color of the western sky before the blizzard rolls in. It was bound in a long, neat braid. The lines on his face were many. Wrinkles surrounded his smile.

I savored the moment.

Like a silent movie, the mouths moved, and there was laughter. I could see it, but I could not hear it. When the laughter subsided, Joe looked at the window and his smile returned. His hand left a dented tin coffee cup, and he waved at me. Time paused. Then he turned to his wife, and they talked some more.

Slowly I was pulled back. Then faster, and the scene began to get distant. I fought to swim back to the window, but I was swept, moaning, away.

"Bones . . . Bones . . . *Bones*! Wake up, darling," Martha said, shaking me gently. "You were dreaming again."

She nestled me to her bosom, still beautiful, her fingers stroking my thinning hair. "Are you all right?" she asked, her eyes soft as the words. I gazed back at her, rose up, and kissed her gently like I have a hundred thousand times.

My heart was still pounding, but I was all right.

More than all right, really.

I am where I should be.

As the years passed, I wondered if it had really been Maya's trail that was leading away from me or if it was my trail that was turning to Martha all along. I wondered if all those years without her were wasted.

We got such a late start.

She says she wasn't waiting for me. She won't admit to that. And I won't admit that she was the reason I came back to Pale Butte. It's a little game we play.

She never resented—not outwardly, anyway—the Christmas cards from Maya and that I kept her in my heart. She did not resent that I held so many others in my heart with her. She did not harrumph when I talked about the old days and the summer of 1977. She encouraged me to keep the memory alive.

"Tell the story," she said. "You know how people are. In a hundred years, no one will believe it happened. They won't believe anything special happened at all."

It's true. After a while, folks got used to Coop's healings down at St. Joseph's Chapel, and when miracles become commonplace, they cease to be viewed as miracles. It's a pity, really.

The sun rises each morning, and I hardly miss a one because I still see it as a miracle. At sunset I witness the glory.

Part of me is waiting, just waiting, to see the sun zip backward in the sky. I laugh to myself when I think of it happening. I'm too old to be scared anymore.

The tall grass rustles. Bugs rub their wings and crickets chirp in applause to the sunset. And I still dance the Ghost Dance. Just a skinny old white man with creaky knees and long white hair dancing on the hill at sunset as I was taught.

I am the last Ghost Dancer.

I dance for Joe Big Cloud.

I wear the Ghost Shirt.

I dance for a better world.

I wear the Ghost Shirt.

I dance for you.

Today as I danced, a line of tumbleweeds appeared from the north, rolling with a giddy sort of military precision. They rose up from a coulee. The line stopped and seemed to watch as two tumbleweeds moved toward me and swirled, dancing with the wind. They reminded me of Joe and Maya. After they had twirled together for a moment, the dancing tumbleweeds led the others away. They rolled away like life rolls away.

I finished the dance and felt the chill as the sun sank behind Pale Butte.

I shivered.

The wind was picking up.